T0196184

HELLFIRE

THE HARVEST

RODNEY GREEN SR.

HELLFIRE
THE HARVEST

iUniverse books may be ordered through booksellers or by contacting:

iUniverse
1663 Liberty Drive
Bloomington, IN 47403
www.iuniverse.com
1-800-Authors (1-800-288-4677)

ISBN: 978-1-4917-7894-4 (sc)
ISBN: 978-1-4917-7893-7 (e)

Library of Congress Control Number: 2015915993

Print information available on the last page.

iUniverse rev. date: 11/12/2015

FOREWORD

I guess because I love to read so much I thought I would try my luck at writing. It was suggested to me, to begin by writing short stories or poems. I think it takes a certain skill to write poetry—a skill I now feel I do not possess. Instead, I decided to write a play first. The play is entitled, *Flawed*, which deals with the struggles of addiction and HIV. Although it is completed, I have not decided whether or not to publish it. I believe I will some day. But for now, I will just be satisfied knowing that the 'select' few I chose to critique it found the play satisfying. Some of their criticism allowed me to go back to add a few things here or there—places in the play I also found myself wondering about. So, to all my critics I say thanks for the tremendous feedback.

Let us talk about Satan. For me, it has always been a fascination—an obsession how people view this principle. Some have called it a concept. I guess one of the biggest questions on the minds of people is—is there a heaven and a hell—and if there is, then what happens to those who are condemned to serve in hell? There are so many descriptions, interpretations, and views but, no real answers. I think the one thing that really troubles me is how some will say *Satan is just something man has created but will say God is real.* Does that mean God Himself, is a creator of fiction? I can just imagine the look on some of the reader's faces in regards to that last line. It is probably the same look my mother—a Christian—gave me when I tried that question on her.

I feel I should give you a fair warning. I love to debate on topics of special interest—preferably, topics which concede to the dogmatic view of others. I feel I should tell you that I am a believer. But I also believe that Satan is more than just a principle. Satan is real and rightly so. I remember watching, *King of Kings*, and Mary—the mother of Jesus told Mary Magdalene, "Evil exists so that we may be the better for it." That phrase, I strongly believe to be as true as the truth can be—a prophetic enlightenment even.

So, one day at home with little to do I sat down, sharpened some pencils, pulled out my binder, and began writing, *Flawed*. It took me several years to complete this play. I hit many snags and mental blocks—not to mention working two jobs—one part time—and attending school and trying to raise an eleven year-old—now an adult.

After the completion of, *Flawed*, I began writing, *The Con*, the third story in this book. I wrote about twelve pages, trashing about half of them and changing the premise entirely. At the time I was reading, *Deception Point*, by Dan Brown, *The Glorious Appearing*, by LaHaye and Jenkins, and, *Piercing the Darkness*, by Frank E. Peretti. I do believe it was a combination of them all which inspired me to change the direction in writing this compilation of short stories.

I intentionally wrote these stories with no happy endings—with no interference or influence from the Father. I felt a book—condemning people to hell cannot in good conscience, be given a happy ending. But I needed to include the possibility of a happy ending.

And so, these five stories depict Satan at his worst—doing what he does best—Deceiving man and woman by convincing them they stand a better chance at hitting the lottery than making it into heaven. And rightly so, I believe. But many disagree with this satanic view—if it is, in fact, a satanic view.

Consider this point if you will: if a man or woman does evil but repents are they truly forgiven? Always? If the answer to that is yes, then where would someone like Adolf Hitler go if, in his final moments, repented and asked God to forgive him? Would he have a place in heaven alongside of Mother Theresa and Dr. Martin Luther King? A frightening thought if you were to ask me.

I chose to write just five stories to match the five positions in hell. And although one story already gives you a clue to the position one character will earn, my job is to make you see why. Choosing the five occupations were a little tricky but I narrowed it down to the five professions you almost always read about in a newspaper or see on the television daily. My next novel will spot an IT geek and an Army General.

I would like to thank my family for the support they have always given me through the years. Also, to my friends and the Trenton folks who have encouraged me to put some of these crazy ideas down on paper. Finally,

I would like to thank the publishers for giving me a chance at getting my feet wet with my first (and definitely not my last) book.

Happy reading,
Rodney Green Sr.

"There the workers of iniquity have fallen;
They have been cast down and are not
able to rise."

PSALM 36:12

CHAPTER 1

There are many tools one can use to seduce others; sex works great; money even greater. But sometimes you just have to look deep to emotions and feelings. Knowing the things which motivate people are extremely advantages for anyone—it was extremely advantages to me. Like many others before Jeremy, I became instrumental in their falls from grace. I needed each one to formulate and put my plan into action—to rule earth and one day, overthrow heaven itself.

I've known Jeremy Smith since he was twelve but did not formally introduce myself until he was twenty. I followed his humble beginnings and from time to time, ran some interference in creating the young man who would one day, become the one known as, "The Griffin."

Jeremy Smith was born and raised on the north side of Trenton. Jeremy was an excellent student and an above average athlete—especially baseball. He was what the neighborhood grown-ups would classify as, "One of the good ones." He was always neat, polite, and very respectful to others. He loved to laugh and had a winning smile with dimples deep enough, to place marbles in them. Because he was from a family of six, times were always hard and Jeremy's only real worry was whether or not there would be enough to eat from day to day.

As I stated before, Jeremy was a good student—always on the honor roll and having a love for science and mathematics. But what he never showed others is the shame he felt. Shame because his father packed up and left when he was ten, leaving his mother to raise and provide for herself and her six children.

Shame because his mother had to concede to county welfare—it was the only way she could provide medical and dental care for her children. It was the only way the family could survive.

As a result of these conditions little Jeremy worked hard in school and at home, helping his mother as best he could. He did, however, hate and

despise his father—two more emotions I will use against Jeremy when the time comes.

Hate, shame, pride, mistrust, and resentment powered by a little ambition and encouragement were the ingredients needed in creating, "The Griffin."

CHAPTER 2

Jeremy Smith, now eighteen—graduated from high school in the top eight percent of his class—is preparing to go to Boston to attend the university where he will be majoring in Chemistry. Because of the mixture of races in his neighborhood he had not really come face to face with true racism. Sure, he had heard about it and even saw it on television, but nothing that was ever the, "In your face," kind of racism. In Boston—in 1983—he would get a small taste of it.

After registering for his classes, Jeremy decided to take another tour of the grounds to familiarize him with the many different buildings, lecture halls, the dining hall, and finally, the library. While going into the library one afternoon, three white students were coming out.

Respectfully, Jeremy held the door for them—considering he had gotten there first—while balancing his books in his left arm. The three students were grinning as they came through. The last one—tall with choppy, blonde hair—intentionally bumped Jeremy's arm, knocking his books on the ground. All three students laughed, as did some of the onlookers. Embarrassed and mildly annoyed, Jeremy said, "I would appreciate it if you picked them up. That was rude and unnecessary."

"Pick them up yourself, nigger!" snapped the blonde headed student.

Calmly, Jeremy put the last book down and replied, "Oh, it's gonna be like that, huh? I know what you want, you jerk! Come and get it!"

The blonde headed student grinned and moved towards Jeremy. As I stated before—Jeremy was extremely athletic. The blonde haired student moved in closer and took a big swing, missing Jeremy and scraping his knuckles against the library door. Jeremy then moved in, throwing a hard right uppercut, catching the student squarely under his chin, and followed it with a left hook which caught his opponent beneath his right eye, creating a nice gash, causing the student to fall back into the crowd which had begun to form. Jeremy began to move in to finish his opponent when

campus security jumped in and separated the two of them. The blonde haired student yelled, "This aint' over yet, nigger! Not by a long shot!"

Blood began to flow more rapidly now. The blonde haired guy pressed a handkerchief below his eye and even spat a little blood on the ground. Apparently, the blow to his chin caused him to bite his tongue also.

When Jeremy saw this all he could do was smile. This angered the student more and even campus security found it a little disturbing and uncalled for. Campus security then escorted Jeremy—rather rudely, perhaps—to the security station, telling the onlookers to go about their business.

At the station, Jeremy was escorted to a room and was forced into a chair. Jeremy found it uncomfortable and difficult to sit still with his adrenaline still peaking. He had never been in trouble before.

A heavy set officer came into the room, holding a legal pad, sat down across from Jeremy and pulled a pen from his left pocket.

"Let's see your school identification, boy," the officer said indignantly.

"Why am I the only one here? I didn't even start the fight. If that jerk didn't ..."

The officer interrupted Jeremy's plea, pounding his fist on the desk. "You don't ask the questions here, I do!"

Startled, Jeremy pulled out his wallet and handed the officer his identification. The officer copied the information he needed, made a copy of the identification, and tossed it back to Jeremy in a Frisbee fashion. Jeremy trapped the identification on his chest, looked at the officer disapprovingly, and returned the document to his wallet. The officer got up, gave him a hard look, and left the room.

As a result, Jeremy was handed a citation for the incident, ordering him to report to the Dean's office that following Monday.

When all was said and done, Jeremy was placed on academic probation while nothing was done to the other student. This was just one of the many times he would have to fight or be humiliated. By the end of the semester, he was kindly asked, by the Dean of Student Affairs, to leave the institution.

CHAPTER 3

Jeremy returned to Trenton, partially defeated and embarrassed that he could not make things work while residing in Boston. The only way he would be able to 'save face', would involve telling his friends how racist the entire town was and how the other blacks there had no real backbone. Having to work in a factory—like many of his friends, who had not even graduated high school—infuriated him. Intellect had been replaced with hate and aggression. It was only a matter of time before the animal would be loosed upon the town of Trenton.

One day while hanging out in the park, Jeremy, along with some friends were sitting on the bleachers, drinking some beer and talking the usual trash to each other. Their discussion of sports was interrupted by a group of young men on the hill, arguing—the kind of arguing which sooner or later lead to a fight.

Jeremy and his friends trotted up the hill to take a closer look—to get a better seat—hopefully something ringside. As they came closer Jeremy recognized one of them. The young man's real name was Mack but a lot of people called him, 'Trees,' a nickname he inherited because he sold a lot of marijuana. Mack had connections with some Jamaican fellows from 145th Street in New York.

Needless to say, the fight never took place—not with Mack and the other guy who went by the name of Ray. Ray was a guy known for, "selling wolf tickets," pretending he wanted to get physical over the price he was being charged for an ounce of pot.

Still intent on talking trash, Ray turned to the growing crowd, inviting anybody to speak up, if they had a problem with him. Well, Jeremy had a problem—a problem with people who ran their mouths too much.

"Man, you talk a lot of shit, and you never do anything!" Jeremy barked.

Ray turned to Jeremy and began sizing him up. Both Ray and Jeremy were of equal height, giving Ray a slight weight advantage and three years

of age on his side. Jeremy was, unfortunately for Ray, more physically fit and talented when it came to fighting.

"So, you wanna jump your punk-ass in my business, huh, motherfucker!" Ray said angrily. "Westside don't back down from you north side bitches!"

Jeremy handed the quart of Colt 45 to his boy and walked up to Ray. "All I have to say to you and your Westside boys is, come and get it."

At that very instant, Ray stepped forward and took a big swing at Jeremy. Jeremy swerved to his right, Ray's fist barely glancing Jeremy's left ear. There's one problem with swinging with all your might; when you miss, your balance is off and you are vulnerable to the counter-punch.

Jeremy came up with a short right upper-cut, thrown as crisp as any trained amateur fighter. There was a loud, "Clap," as the punch caught Ray directly beneath his chin, forcing his lower jaw to crash into his upper jaw. This is one of the reasons a fighter learns to breathe through his nose and keep his mouth shut because that punch sent streams of lightning into Ray's brain, temporarily disrupting all neural connections. Ray dropped straight down on his knees. His eyes were glassy as if he was staring out into some empty space. Jeremy then took a quick, short step back and brought everything he had in a left hook which caught ray on the right side of his temple, propelling Ray sideways, with him ending in a semi-fetal position.

Jeremy then turned to the guys who were with Ray, with fists balled tightly and a look in his eyes—a look which told the others how easily they could share Ray's fate.

Ray's guys backed off, some shaking their heads indicating they wanted no part of what Jeremy was offering. Jeremy turned and regrouped with his friends. As they were walking through the crowd, some of those gathered, whispered things like, "Man, did you see that?" and, "That kid can thump." One girl said, "Do you think he killed him? That guy's not moving at all." Dead or alive, Jeremy could care less. He was not the type of guy who would stand for anyone getting aggressive with him—provoked or not.

A few days pass when Jeremy was approached by Mack." Jeremy, at that time was leaning on his friend, Darrell's car, listening to the radio while munching on some French fries. The guys all looked at Mack as he strolled over.

"Yo', what's up Jeremy?"

"Nothing much bro, what's up with you?"

"I just wanted to talk to you about something … in private."

Jeremy gives the last of his fries to Pete who quickly leaps into the basket as if he had not eaten in days. "Damn boy, slow ya' ass down before you choke," replied Darrell. Jeremy and Mack walk away from the car.

Mack begins the conversation by saying, "I wanna talk to you about that fight the other day." Mack is unsure how to really approach Jeremy on the subject but realizes he has already opened the door. "Well, it's like this … how you wound up fighting Ray instead of me or even one of my boys, I don't really know. The truth is … that punk didn't really want to fight … he's the kind that talks the talk. Anyway, I just wanted to let you know I appreciated how you stood up for me like that. That shit was real."

"I stood up more for north side, than you," Jeremy casually replied. "Besides, I hate guys that think a little cussing is gonna scare people."

"Okay, so you did it for the honor of north side. Tell me something … is honoring all you are willing to fight for?"

"What else is there?" Jeremy inquired.

"Well, there's money, power, and respect, to name a few."

"Never gave any of that shit much thought … except the respect part."

"So, why do it for respect alone? That shit can't feed nobody."

"You mean anybody. That shit cannot feed anybody."

"I almost forgot you're a college boy."

"I used to be a college boy … now, I just don't know."

"So, why don't we get down to some real business," Mack says confidently. "I would like to use your services … to watch the backs of some of my boys while they're on the block. You don't have to sell or even touch the stuff … just make sure no one tries to hassle them."

"I already have a job … thanks but no thanks."

"Don't be so quick to say no, dude. You may not even have to lift a finger especially, after putting Ray in a coma with two punches. Customers will think twice about causing any static with Mark and you on the block."

"That's why God created guns … to shoot those you can't beat. Besides, you can't pay too much for protecting your smoke."

"And that would be true if that were all I sold. I don't want you to watch the weed sellers. I need you to watch out for the coke and dope

dealers. A few hours a night is all I'm asking. Give it a shot and if you don't like the job, you can quit."

Jeremy knew those guys selling the powder made decent—maybe more than decent, money. And if he's not touching or selling it, he could easily walk away if things got too hot.

"Tell you what, Mack ... give me a few days to think this through. I will get back to you with an answer."

"That's cool with me. Besides, if you just jumped on board, I would have to question this whole north side honor stuff you were preachin'. You know where to find me when you come to a decision. See you later."

Jeremy goes back to the car. Darrell, Pete, and Marshall are already inside waiting for him. He gets in and the car pulls off to the sound of, "My Radio," by L.L. Cool J.

CHAPTER 4

A few days pass and Jeremy decides to join Mack's organization—to keep an eye open for the dealers and occasionally, control the crowd. As Mack had foretold, rarely did Jeremy have to flex his muscle to anyone; hearing the news of Jeremy putting a man in a two-week coma makes a person think twice before starting trouble. When Jeremy wasn't watching the backs of the dealers, he was usually with Mack making sure no one approached him with any animosity.

One day while at his usual post—sitting at the top of the bleachers watching the dealers peddle—Jeremy observed the kids in the nearby baseball field practicing. The infielders were running drills, the outfielders were located between center and left field catching, "pop flies," and in the right field the pitchers and catchers were warming up.

The pitching coach looked over and noticed Jeremy watching the pitchers. The coach remembered, so long ago, that Jeremy was once a star in this park. He walked over to the fence where Jeremy, was now standing.

"Brings back a lot of memories, doesn't it?"

Jeremy turned his gaze from the pitchers and remembered this coach from the days he used to play baseball here. "It brings back too many memories," Jeremy replied, with a slight smile.

"If I recall correctly, you were quite a decent pitcher. You were one of the best to come through here … a twelve-year-old with an arsenal of pitches.

"Yes, I was pretty good back then. Baseball was so much fun then. No college scouts, no jealous teammates or coaches who showed favoritism to color, and no politics."

"That is one of the reasons I still coach little league—teaching the lads to have fun—basic *fundamentals*. I still remember that game you pitched against the Yankees—seventeen strikeouts in one game—a record that still remains here."

"Only because the eighteenth and final out was a fly ball back to me ... I made all eighteen outs that day."

"Makes a person wonder why anyone would waste such a talent selling drugs," the coach says, rather sharply.

"I don't sell drugs and no one sells drugs for me. I just hang around and try to keep the peace around here. That is no different from a bouncer in a titty-bar."

"Sounds like semantics to me but you dress it up any way you like, ace. But it does not change a thing. Your job is to protect and guard someone else's investment ... like some sort of Gryphon."

"Excuse me, a what?"

"A Gryphon ... a mystical creature ... half eagle and half lion used to guard treasure; many stories praised the Gryphon on its strength and ferocity—From the Achaemenid Persian Empire to Central Asia. That figure is still used today at libraries, cathedrals, and museums ... anywhere there are treasures in need of protection."

"Are you calling me an animal?" Jeremy expressed angrily.

"Those are your words, not mine. But like the Gryphon, people say you are just as fierce and formidable except the Gryphon is a protector *from* evil."

"Careful coach or you may just see how fierce I can be."

"I'm not here to preach to you and I sure don't want to make you angry. But when we talk to these young people at the training facility they see the 'Wall of Fame' and they see *your* picture there. That wall is in place for one reason ... to inspire these young men. So, what do you think these boys say when they see one of their heroes out here doing what you do?"

"Do you really think I give two shits what these boys think? I could care less."

"Then why does it upset you so? For someone who doesn't care, you have a funny way of showing it."

Jeremy looks back to the dealers by the basketball court and the two at the top of the hill, hoping this little distraction will allow him a moment to regroup. His mind tells him the coach is right but his anger—for how unfairly he feels he has been treated—will not afford him rational thought. He has no justification to offer the coach.

"Well, it's obvious you have a job to do and so do I, so I will leave you to your work … and your thoughts," the coach says emphatically. "Take care … Gryphon."

The coach walks away, never looking back leaving Jeremy to his thoughts.

Griffin … it shall be.

CHAPTER 5

It is a typically warm summer day at Martin Luther King Jr. Park. The playground is located northeast of the basketball courts—separated by the Al Downing Little League Baseball field. The playground is full—children occupying every swing, slide, and monkey-bar available. The public swimming pool is adjacent to the left and left-centerfield of the ball park. The sounds of laughter—splashing and the occasional whistle blowing by the lifeguards, reminding the swimmers to walk and stop running. The ballpark is silent now but will be alive much later when the sun is no longer peaking. The basketball courts however, are full with guys playing five-on-five full court and many guys on the sidelines, awaiting their chance at the winners.

With so many out and about the dealers find it quite easy to blend in and conduct the usual business. Jeremy, now known to everyone in the neighborhood as, "The Griffin," conducts his normal routine of going from one site to the other, checking in with the dealers, being assured all is well. Jeremy also observes every person in the area—checking out those who may be, "Peeping," where the dealers hide their packages.

After about an hour and twenty minutes of conducting business, one of the lookouts yell, "Five-O,"—a term alerting the dealers the cops were in the vicinity. Hearing the warning, the dealers' job is simple; leave the stash where it is and calmly walk away from it, as far as possible. Sometimes the cops do find the drugs, but rarely, can they pin the abandoned drugs on anyone. Most of the time, the cops glance right over the spot where the drugs are hidden and return to their patrol cars empty handed. They prefer to actually catch someone with the product instead of having to write a report on, 'Phantom dope'. Today should have been one of them days when they settled on finding the drugs with no one to pin them on; if they had, no one would have had to die.

The cops—Trenton's finest—had come through like clockwork and began the usual routine of checking the brick wall at the top of the hill,

the shrubbery, and honeysuckle bushes at the backyard of one of the neighboring houses, and a few parked cars on Burton Avenue, which runs parallel to the basketball courts. While the cops conducted their searches, the dealers casually walked away in different directions.

The Griffin, now on the bleachers enjoying a ginger ale and pretending to watch the boys play ball, cautiously observed—looking to see if any of the stash sites were discovered. None of them were—not by the cops, anyway.

A junkie, well-known by the dealers also noticed the cops' failure to uncover the hidden drugs. When the police returned to their cars and pulled off, the junkie casually strode pass one of the stash spots, bent down, and turned over a fairly large stone, revealing the brown paper bag containing about six hundred dollars worth of product. The junkie quickly stuffed the bag in his sock, fixed the bottom of his jeans, and stood up, pretending to have found a coin. He quickly pulled some change from his pocket and added the new coin to the fold—counting and recounting the change as he walked towards the alley perpendicular to Bond Street.

When the Griffin saw this he could not believe it. *Did he really do what I think he did?* The Griffin had to be sure. He went to the top of the hill and walked past the spot, pretending to check his pager and noticed the rock had been turned over; the contents—once concealed by the rock—now gone.

After reporting this news to Mack, the Griffin left Mack's apartment and jumped in the passenger side of a red Honda. "The Westside," he said to his driver.

Arriving at the Westside of Trenton a few minutes past seven, Jeremy and the driver went to a nearby liquor store on Prospect Street, purchased a quart of beer and a pack of Newport's, returned to the car and headed further west to Stuyvesant Avenue. There, they parked the car and decided to wait. Jeremy grew angry with every passing minute. He could not remember the last time he was so angry.

About forty minutes later the waiting paid off. The house across the street where they parked seemed to be getting a little traffic—mostly low-bottom junkies, shuffling in and out of the establishment. Then they spotted their target. He had come to the front door. He gave some guy money to run to the store to pick something up. Looking around and

flashing a handful of one and five dollar bills like some big shot and counting them as if they were hundreds. The junkie went back inside, locking the door.

The Griffin and the driver looked at each other smirking. "What a fucking idiot," the driver said, popping a magazine into the butt of a .25 caliber semi-automatic handgun.

"Just keep the engine running and get out if needed," replied the Griffin.

The Griffin got out of the car and proceeded across the street, carrying a sawed-off 12-gauge shotgun—double-barreled. He went up the steps and knocked at the door.

The junkie came to the door, assuming it was the guy he just sent to the store, and opened the door without checking first. He opened the door and tried to slam it shut. But it was way too late for that. Jeremy grabbed the junkie by the collar and pulled him out on the porch.

Before he could attempt to apologize—before he could even go into his pockets and try to give the money or what was left of the product back—the Griffin held the shotgun up to the junkie's face and squeezed the trigger.

The sound was deafening—both barrels were unloaded on the junkie taking most of his head completely off, splattering blood, bone, and gray matter on the porch, railing, and windows. This was Jeremy's first kill. Something shifted inside him—something he had not felt in a really, long time. It was something he had been missing. It was orgasmic. It was a satisfaction, slightly short of pure bliss.

The Griffin then, casually walked down the steps, crossed the street, and jumped in the car, with the driver pulling off before the Griffin could even fully, close the door. Passersby, mostly junkies themselves, ran up on the porch and began sifting through the dead man's pockets, taking everything—stained or not—and going on about their own business. In the house, across the street from this execution, a figure stands in the window videotaping the entire incident.

CHAPTER 6

The summer is almost over and it's business as usual. Even with the many rumors floating around about the Griffin and how he executed someone in broad daylight with absolute impunity; no cops, no investigation; nothing was done regarding this matter. Did anyone care? The guy was just a junkie—the lowest of the low. Anyway, as a result of this, no one would ever dare try and take off Mack's crew again. No one wanted to face the wrath of, "The Griffin." Besides, during this time it was not easy obtaining weapons unless you knew someone who knew someone. And the Griffin had found something he had been missing in his life. Murder has now, become his addiction.

With summer winding down the park is beginning to clear out—no more swimming or baseball. And the swings, sliding boards, and monkey bars have become almost abandoned now. However, the basketball courts are still operational so the dealers can continue to blend in. The basketball courts will probably remain occupied until the first snowfall.

CHAPTER 7

Mack's main distributor is indicted on multiple drug charges and will not be released from jail for the next thirty-five years. Mack and his crew are meeting a new supplier today. This man once lived in Cuba but has been in the U.S. for about four years. This is a man who has established quite a reputation—a ruthless one. Rumor has it, Alejandro, "King," Gomez loves to torture, dismember, and sometimes, burn his victims. Mack would rather deal with someone else but this new supplier gives the best deal on the entire east coast. All will remain well provided loyalty is maintained and business continues to flow with a high degree of consistency. As for the Griffin, he has developed a taste for killing—sometimes doing it out of fun and not necessarily—out of necessity. This undoubtedly, pleases me.

Six months pass and it's a cold day in February. Business has been good—too good as rival dealers on the south and eastside are continually feeling a big pinch in their pockets. Most of the dealers can no longer compete with Mack and his boys from the north side especially, since they have to buy their goods from a New York supplier. Blood is spilled throughout Trenton and surrounding neighborhoods. Both south and eastside arrange a meeting to discuss a permanent solution to all their problems. They meet on neutral territory—the deepest and most secluded section of Mill Hill Park, located in the downtown section of Trenton. A compromise is made; however, Mack, the Griffin, and his north side boys would continue to have the advantage and a more secure and untouchable supplier.

CHAPTER 8

It's Valentine's Day and Mack is taking his girlfriend to a show in Philadelphia, but first, dinner at Carmela's favorite spot—Amici Milano's located in the Chambersburg section of Trenton.

Mack earlier disregarded the Griffin's suggestion to change things up and dine elsewhere—possibly in Philly. He also requested that either he or Mark accompany Mack and Carmela as a chauffeur or chaperone. But Mack assured the Griffin things would go fine. And besides, he needed the Griffin to oversee the latest shipment of product. Mack tells the Griffin he always felt the pick-ups go more smoothly with him present. And that he trusts no one else to handle his affairs in his absence. The Griffin concedes to Mack's request.

Mack and Carmela enjoy a lovely dinner at her favorite restaurant especially, dessert—a tiramisu made from scratch.

Mack pays the check and he and Carmela leave the restaurant. The valet takes his ticket and brings the car around—a 1988 Cadillac Seville—black with soft, cream leather interior and shiny spoked rims.

The couple gets into the car and makes a k-turn to avoid going out of the way of their next destination. They pull up to the light on Chestnut Avenue, listening to the music and awaiting the light to change. A car slows through the light and stops, blocking Mack's car. Another car quickly pulls in behind Mack. Two men exit each car and run up to Mack's car. Flashing lights and the sound of automatic gunfire erupts, shattering the windshield, side windows, and peppering the driver's door. Fifteen seconds later, both cars head down Chestnut Avenue, leaving Mack and Carmela at the light—dead.

The Griffin and the rest of the crew receive the news at about 2:30 that morning. They assemble at the apartment of Mack's cousin Terry. Terry asks the boys to make inquiries while he breaks the news to his Aunt Belinda—Mack's mom. Terry will have to go with his aunt to identify the

body while the Griffin and the others hit the streets hoping that someone will run their mouth and provide a little information for them.

Several days pass and they are burying Mack. I do not attend the funeral or the burial site. Instead, I decide to meet with the Griffin at the reception which followed. I walk over to the Griffin, lean down to whisper something in his ear. The Griffin replies with a whisper of his own. Once that is completed, I depart while the Griffin goes over to Mark and informs him a meeting has been arranged and that he should attend it. Mark tells the Griffin, "I'm out man for good, this time. The crew is now in your hands."

As those in attendance begin leaving the Mack's family home one of the crew members walk up to the Griffin asking, "What happens now? Who's gonna take over?" The Griffin tells him to get the crew together and meet him at the spot by the park. The Griffin walks to his car with my words of encouragement still pinging in his head. *The show must go on … and it will.*

CHAPTER 9

Apropos, no one ever laid a claim to killing Mack and so no more inquiries are made at this time. The crew wanted to just go out and blast a few sections but the Griffin knew that action would inevitably, bring unnecessary heat on them. Besides, the Griffin felt if there are conspicuous killings, they will be by his hand and his hand alone. The Griffin, accompanied by Singi, will meet with me to determine the next move. Hopefully, this meeting will prevent a full scale war, still pending.

The Griffin and Singi drive to a spot in New Brunswick called, "El Palacio." The Griffin found it ironic that the, "King," would own a restaurant with that name.

They walked in and as they suspected, were met by four men, obviously strapped, who began the ritual of patting them down. Once their weapons were removed, the Griffin was instructed to go through the double doors while Singi, would have to cool his heels in a booth located at the rear of the restaurant.

The Griffin continues to walk down a long corridor with his escort a few feet in front of him. The escort speaks with a heavy Latin accent into a walkie-talkie. At the end of the corridor there's a huge, heavy-looking metal door. The Griffin hears a loud, "click," indicating the door is being unlocked. The door opens and the Griffin follows the escort inside. *El Palacio is right* the Griffin thinks as he walks inside. The room opens up into something which resembles a nicely decorated, airplane hangar. Six foot pictures and murals on the walls, statues; some on pedestals, and at least a half dozen area rugs measuring 14'x 18' easily. To the right of this huge room was a large round below ground tub which could comfortably fit twenty people. There were four beautiful women in the tub frolicking in the bubbles. To the left, a long, solid cherry table, large enough to accommodate a twenty person committee—if need be.

The Griffin notices a figure sitting at the end of the long table and immediately walks over to me.

"Welcome Griffin," I said, invitingly. "Come—have a seat. I will have someone bring us food and drink."

The Griffin takes a seat on the side of the table so his back would not be at the door. "Bravo Senor, you are careful and cautious of your surroundings but respectful. I like that in a man and business associate."

A couple gentlemen dressed in all white approach with assorted seafood, wine, beer, and a box of authentic Cubans. They carefully place the items on the table, with the cigars in the front corner facing me.

"That will be all for now."

The waiters quietly return from whence they came.

I begin by saying, "Once again, I am terribly saddened by the loss of Mack. He was a young man whom I found … how do you say it … true to the game?"

The Griffin acknowledges the sentiment with a short nod.

"Am I correct in assuming you and your men have yet to discover those responsible?"

"We've decided to leave the matter alone … for now. We feel we need to see where we stand with you. War would harm the business more than it would help. And besides, sooner or later someone will talk. They always do."

"Before we get down to business, I suggest we drop the formalities. You may call me Alex. And what shall I call you?"

"Griffin is okay with me. I rarely use my real name."

"Griffin, it shall be. Now, I think it only wise I tell you this before we begin. It was recently brought to my attention the south side boys met with the boys from the eastside.

They conspired to take out Mack. And their plan was obviously, a successful one. If I had to guess—I would say the south side boys actually pulled the trigger."

The Griffin leans forward, placing both hands flat on the table. "And just why, would you think south side pulled the trigger?"

"Do the math, Senor. The south side has more to lose with Mack alive, and more to gain with him dead. They knew that his 'connect'—namely myself—would find them not to exact revenge but to place Mack's commitment and debt on them. This is what they are still hoping on."

The Griffin had once considered all this but felt even if it were true—the south side boys would still require some backing—and possibly permission to carry it out. The Griffin decided to keep this thought to him—for now.

"As I said before … we will make no moves towards anyone … for now."

"That, my friend is fine with me," I replied. "Besides, anymore blood baths on the street will prove unprofitable to all. Now … down to the real business. You guys on the north have lost your leader. It is clear to everyone that you are the best and only choice for the job. I am prepared to make the exact same guarantee to you as I made with Mack. But, you have to offer me something extra … a little insurance, so to speak. I fashioned, tutored, and molded Mack for years and you my friend, will have to take a crash course in business administration and finance."

"And just what kind of insurance is that?" The Griffin inquired.

"I want your oath … in blood."

"You want my what?" Jeremy asked confused.

"My apologies, Senor … I believe in the spiritual and spirits—unseen forces which connect people on a level far greater than a man's word or handshake. Blood creates a more … unbreakable bond. Simply put, I would be willing to die for you and you for me. And if something should happen to any of us, the other *must* exact revenge. This is something I never felt I needed to do with Mack. He was too 'street' for that. But you, my friend, well, you are different. For this oath, I will give you some strong, political connections … lawyers, judges, politicians, and all the crooked cops you need."

After giving all I said some thought Jeremy asked, "So, how does this, 'blood thing,' work?"

CHAPTER 10

The Griffin joins forces with me and pledges his blood; in life as well as in death. As an act of faith, I made inquiries, had those responsible for Mack's death rounded up and delivered to an abandoned warehouse out on the East State Street Extension near Mercerville. This area was comprised of factories, salvage yards, a textile mill and assorted small businesses. The Griffin, along with his crew was invited to witness the inquisition. Once, enough of them confessed to the why and how, my men began the ritual of purification—soaking the men in gasoline and listening to them plead for their pathetic lives—scratching and trying to climb out of the man-made pit they had been placed in. The Griffin and his now, right hand man Marshall, stood at the edge of the pit and observed it all.

I hold a torch out to the Griffin, allowing him to do the honors. The Griffin takes the torch and says, "Hell has reserved a place for all of you." The Griffin takes one serious look at the torch and tosses it into the pit.

Screams of agony and wails of torment reverberate throughout the warehouse. Some of the Griffin's crew turns their faces in disgust while my crew grins with eyes that seem to dance to the rhythm of the flickering flames, casting a hellish silhouette throughout the room. This, my crew have witnessed before. The screams of the men appear to continue, long after the last body is but ashes.

The Griffin then turns to me. "I want the ashes placed in three jars. One will go to the Southside, one to the eastside and the third I will deliver personally."

"And to whom will you be delivering those ashes to my friend?"

"Those ashes will be a gift to Mack's cousin Terry. I think he will appreciate knowing Mack's killers didn't get away."

I now look on Jeremy with an increased, pleasing approval. "Cunio, I should have thought of that."

CHAPTER 11

The next year went in the manner as promised. The Griffin was feared more than ever—not because of how ruthless he had become—but more in the way his connections had strengthened. Police gave him tips when someone was trying to move in on his operations. Certain judges made sure the Griffin would appear before them if he had to appear in court.

And he had Theodore Harding—the best criminal lawyer on the east coast. The Griffin had become untouchable. A cop, employed by yours truly approached him one evening to give him a warning.

"What can I do for you, officer?" Griffin asked.

"It turns out you have an uninvited guest joining your party tomorrow night. He's an undercover cop, on loan from Boston."

"Did you say Boston? Our friend is from Boston? Well, it won't pain me any to take out a cat from Boston. Are you sure he's the mole?"

"I got the tip from an extremely reliable source."

"And just how does your source say we play this one?"

"He wants you to just do what it is you do. But we have to give them someone. Someone with a record is preferable."

"Someone like maybe … Johnny T.?"

"Why not, he's the one who brought him in, right?"

"Anything else you need, officer?" asked the Griffin.

"Yeah, change the location to the Lincoln Homes, down by the canal at the bottom of Old Rose Street. Also, do yourself a favor and make the move in his car. You wouldn't want to get that Grand National messy, now would you?"

"No, I wouldn't. Take care and tell your source I really appreciate this. This will not be forgotten. I owe you both, for this."

"Don't mention it. Just remember … I deal in cash only."

Both men laugh as the officer leaves. It always pleases the Griffin when he has an opportunity to settle a score. Jeremy calls one of his men and requests J.T. meet him within the hour. He will send J.T. on a little assignment which will temporarily, separate him from the mole.

CHAPTER 12

I am still at the restaurant in the back conducting business and talking on the phone to a certain lawyer regarding a certain chain of events which took place last night. The intercom on the desk blinks and lightly buzzes. I tell the lawyer I will have to call him back. I press the intercom, asking what the person on the other end wants.

"Boss, there is a Mr. Brennan here to see you."

"Okay, send him in."

Mr. Brennan enters the room. He walks past the pool size bathtub and gazes at the four bikini clad women. They all look up and smile at him.

"Councilman, I'm pretty sure you didn't come all the way up here from Trenton to engage in pleasures of the flesh."

Mr. Brennan snaps out of his lustful gaze and walks over to me, smiling as he pulls up a chair. He looks back at the women one more time, winks, and turns back to me, extending a handshake.

"People usually shake my hand and wait to be seated, councilman. Have we forgotten our manners or are we intentionally being rude?"

"My apologies Alex," Mr. Brennan says respectfully. "You know quite well now how beautiful women affect me. Like, walking by an apple orchard ... you just have to pick one, whether you're hungry or not."

"That's how Eve tricked Adam, David. She simply convinced him there was no harm in one apple and the next thing you know, an eviction notice is served to them."

"I think it's a little too late in the game to feed me scripture, Alex. You and I both know what a waste of time that is to the both of us now."

"Sorry my friend but you know how much I enjoy scripture. It can be a seductively convincing tool. You still remember the one I used on you?"

"Of course I do. You quoted me PSALM 143:2."

"So, you do still remember. Now, how may I help you?"

"I take it you already know what went down last night?"

"Of course I do, why?"

26

"Well, that is a big problem. Your boy needs to have his leash tightened … or yanked or something. He has gone too far with last night's killing. I had over two dozen calls in my office today. I was finally force to call it an early workday."

"Did he not give you and your constituents someone juicy to immolate … an example to be set in support of the death penalty?"

"They want … they need more … someone higher up … nothing less is going to satisfy the masses."

I reach over the table and place both hands on David's, gripping it gently.

"Do not fret over this Davey. All is going according to plan. You already have Mr. Thomas, a three-time loser. And soon, you will have a much bigger fish."

"Are you sure he suspects nothing? That guy's pretty smart you know."

"I believe I'm a lot smarter. Do you agree?"

"Of course I do. And because I do, there was no need to even ask such a question."

"Good. You know very well how I deal with those who are impudent towards me."

"It isn't necessary for you to remind me, master. What should my next move be?"

"Inform your constituents that the trap is set and they will soon have their fish. You will be a shoe-in for Mayor when the term comes around."

"I guess the only appropriate response to that is … it's better to reign in hell than serve in heaven," Mr. Brennan says jovially.

"Hell is mine … Asphodel will be yours. And the Griffin's time on top is about to expire."

CHAPTER 13

It's business as usual for the Griffin and the north side boys. They are now operating on all four corners of the north and have spread out through several parts which were geographically questionable. The Griffin received a hot tip that one of his warehouses had to be hit on the coming Saturday morning so he should move the bulk of his product to another location, leaving DEA a small percentage to hang their hats on. The Griffin then sets up Friday evening as the day to clear the warehouse.

The north side boys are busy—packing the goods and preparing to transfer 87% of the product to another location. A few men are selected to take the fall; to be on the site when the raid takes place. The selected men consider it an honor for they know the Griffin will come through in the end. They know they will do little to no time in prison and will be greatly rewarded. They know they will be treated like kings; in prison and upon their return to the streets.

The Griffin shows up to oversee the final preparations. He checks his watch and looks up at the rectangular, translucent windows. It is getting late—sunlight no longer strains to pierce the glass. Dusk is approaching and the trucks are running late. He is beginning to get a bad feeling; a gnawing at his clandestine sensibility.

Someone then calls out, "The trucks are here." Several men murmur, "It's about time." One guy runs over to the main door and proceeds to unlock the chain which is connected to a pulley. He begins hand over hand, pulling down on the chain which begins to lift the garage door.

Once the door is lifted high enough three large trucks—24 footers— begin pulling in and are directed to different locations within the warehouse. From that point, everything else happened too quickly.

The trucks' back doors fly open and out come dozens of men in riot gear with weapons rose. The north side boys were half frozen as shotguns, M-16's, and assorted hand guns explode in all directions—cutting men down, shattering lights, and peppering walls—as clouds of white dust

began billowing in the air. This only takes about five minutes. The gunfight is over as quickly as it had begun. The north side boys and the Griffin had been caught with their pants down.

The men in riot gear—DEA, ATF, and several U.S. Marshalls—begin checking for any north side survivors. If any are found still alive they are to be terminated on sight. They were, however, instructed to bring the Griffin in alive, if possible.

The Griffin was injured but still willing to put up a fight. Completely surrounded now, the Griffin had been ordered to drop his weapon and surrender. He has no choice now but to concede to the demands given him.

Two men grab him by the arms to escort him to a black Cadillac, which silently, crept in during the chaos. Someone runs to the rear door and opens it. A figure steps out and walks over to the Griffin who is still being assisted by his strong-armed escorts. The Griffin looks the person in the eyes; seeing but not believing what his brain is now trying to convince him of.

"Good evening Senor."

"Alex, what is the meaning of this?"

"Well, it's like this, amigo … you have just recently become more of a liability than an asset. There is a certain politician that I have placed much stock in … an investment in the future of my rule here on earth. I cannot very well get too far with a drug dealer now could I?"

"You used me … used me to help some fucking pedophile?"

"David is not a pedophile, Griffin; he's a pederast … a pederast who will serve a far greater purpose for me than some drug dealer whose life expectancy is that of a common housefly. Face it, my friend, drug dealers don't last long here, in the U.S. You are all allowed to go only so far before we put on the brakes. You all, in the end, make us all heroes. And the American public loves its heroes."

"Is that right … and what about you, Alex? Aren't you a drug dealer … a Kingpin?" "No, not really. It is only what I wanted you to believe me to be … you and you alone. To tell you the truth … I have many occupations and many names. Do you still remember your 'blood oath' to me?"

Jeremy, as hard as he tries, is having difficulty getting his mind to wrap around what is happening to him. He jerks away from his escorts and before they can resume their grip, I raise a hand stopping them. Jeremy

attempts to stand straight but the gunshot wound in his side makes it difficult.

"I must admit a little more truth, Griffin. I have always admired your strength and courage. You could have made a good name for yourself as a foot soldier. You could have even commanded one of my armies. Unfortunately for you, a drug dealers' fate is that of a slave ... nothing more for earth scum like you."

"What in the hell are you talking about? What fucking army?"

"I'm talking about an army of the earth, slave ... my legion. The army I am creating to one day overtake heaven by force."

Jeremy stands there, perplexed and dumbstruck. He is finding it even harder to believe what he is hearing. "Are you telling me that you really are ... that your name is ...?"

"Hard to say, is it not? Like I said before, I am many names and many faces. I congratulate the church for describing me, literally as a beast with horns. Human guises work far better for me than some goat, or serpent."

Jeremy's wound causes him to buckle. He drops to one knee, gripping his side, grimacing from the pain. He looks up to me, still determined to fully understand. "All I have done ... I cannot believe this is how you repay someone ... you and your 'blood oath'."

"You can feel as bad about this as you like, slave. I have defeated and deceived men far greater than you and those who helped get you will soon get theirs. After all, if the scorpion promises not to sting and he in fact, does sting, you cannot blame him for it. After all, he is a scorpion."

"So, what happens now ... what happens to me?"

"You will be arrested, tried for numerous crimes, including the murders of the east and south side boys along with the murder of an undercover agent and that junkie—I had that one videotaped—along with drug trafficking and a violation of the RICO. For all that you will receive the death sentence. Oh yeah, those ashes you wanted delivered ... they were delivered to the FBI. Now that is some serious evidence."

The Griffin attempts to get up—to lunge at me for one last time—to get a few licks in but the men are on him immediately. They handcuff him and drag him off, kicking and screaming.

"Do you think he will try to expose you master ... tell people who you really are?" the driver asks curiously.

"One could only hope. What better way to convince people I do not exist, than to have a murderous drug dealer say I do? Besides, they won't allow him to use the insanity defense to escape the lethal injection. His connections are gone along with his money. He will have to rely on a public defender so he is really screwed."

The driver opens the door, allowing me to step inside. The car pulls off, with me laughing as the car disappears into the night.

Epilogue: Devilish diversion

Okay, I came up a little short with this one … thought I could use Jeremy like a knight or a rook but it turns out, he was only one of many pawns in this chess game. I really did believe he would command one of my armies but now I see he was good for one thing only—to aid in making a name for a certain attorney and a politician you will hear about much later in this series.

"Do not let you heart turn aside to her ways;
Do not stray into her paths;
For she has cast down many wounded,
And all who were slain by her were strong men.
Her house is the way to hell,
Descending to the chambers of death."

Proverbs 7:25-27
The Wiles of a Harlot

CHAPTER 1

I have known of Gabrielle Milos since birth but did not take any real interest in her until the age of ten. Although she was still at that age of innocence, I began putting certain people in place to insure her arrival; that is to say, I did everything in my power to one day, have the privilege of meeting this young lady.

People seem to always say things like, "The devil made me do it," or, "That's the devil in you," which, most of the time is a complete falsehood. But in this case, I have to admit; it was I, who created the girl who would one day be, quite the delightfully, cunning monster I envisioned.

Gabrielle was a delightful little ten-year-old, if there is such a thing. She was neat and respectful; well mannered that is. She was, however, a curious child—sexually curious. She had an obsession with Barbie Dolls—everything the stores sold regarding Barbie—she begged her parents for. So, her parents bought her the camper, corvette, and even Barbie's friends. Gabrielle made sure her Barbie had everything including, a boyfriend. She had her parents go out and buy the Ken doll.

I did mention how curious she was didn't I? Sure, having Barbie and Ken take a ride in the corvette and share a kiss would have been enough for any 12-year-old and would be a rare thing for a 10-year-old. But Gabrielle was different from most little girls. She was *extremely* curious. Some nights she would sneak out of her room to listen in on her parents. The sounds emanating from the room increased her curiosity.

Every now and again she would hear them say, "I love you," which she later connected to the moans and groans of her mother. The other sounds—the light squeaking of the bed, vibration of the walls and bedroom door, and a smell—a strange sweetness which she could not determine their points of origin. That same smell would be there in the morning but not as acute, as the night before. This really raised her curiosity.

Some of Gabrielle's curiosities are about to be satisfied. Her parents had to go out of town so Gabrielle had to stay with her mother's sister, Sarah

still don't understand, do you? I guess I'd better show you what it means."
He removed her clothes and then his own. He then molested her in the
same fashion as he positioned the dolls.

He made Gabrielle promise to never tell anyone and gave her twenty
dollars. He promised her he would buy her anything she ever wanted.
Gabrielle agreed and promised David she would never tell their little secret.
This is how Gabrielle came to be known as, "The Harlot."

CHAPTER 2

Years pass and Gabrielle, now age 16, began sleeping with college boys—for money, of course. She would walk along Kuser Road awaiting that chivalrous and horny lad to pull over and ask to give her a lift. If the car was really nice, she would hop in. She would never deal with high school boys. That way, she would not be known as, 'The Slut'. After all, Gabrielle had managed to keep her professional promiscuity a secret. She still—from time to time—collects her, 'hush money' from good old Uncle David who still remained her first and continuous customer. Gabrielle knew to maintain her advantageous position on him.

Needless to say, Gabrielle was good—really good when it came to pleasing her customers. Secretly, she would watch old Vanessa Del Rio and Alicia Rio films, tutoring her in the ways to satiate others. Gabrielle was meticulous in concealing her private life. And, she could always keep a secret—hers and theirs.

Gabrielle was discreet to the point her parents were completely oblivious to her extracurricular activities.

She managed to open an account in the name of Giselle Milian, a fan dancer from Paris whom she noticed while watching a documentary on the history of erotic dancing. She bribed the vice president of a bank who also became a loyal and extremely regular customer of hers. The vice president set up an account for her—complete with identification, a birth certificate, and even a passport—if she were to ever need it.

Her life at this point was going well; then she met me.

CHAPTER 3

I had the distinct pleasure of meeting Gabrielle one Saturday afternoon while she was shopping. Although she was only sixteen, she had extremely mature taste in clothes. She knew how to dress in a way which made her look older than she was. She could easily pass for a woman of twenty-one but she could also dress in a way which made her a woman younger than her real age. For this look she simply adorned her classic catholic school look, complete with pig tails.

I awaited her return to the parking lot as she approached her car, a forest green Nissan Stanza with specialty plates, 'Sassy', on them. She had a loyal customer down at the DMV who created a fake drivers license and registration. She later changed them over when she met her banker friend. Gabrielle always knew how to move and who to move. Her customers were more than just a means to an end. If there was anything she needed that money alone could not buy, her talent, cunning, and beauty would provide for her.

I approached her as harmless and as casual as I could. "Lovely day, isn't it Ms. Milian … I mean, Ms. Milos?" She looked up slightly startled saying, "How do you know me and who are you?"

"I am a big fan of yours … have been for quite some time."

She carefully placed her bags in the back seat of her car, while keeping a watchful eye on me. I took a step back, keeping my hands to my side, trying to be as less threatening as possible. She closed the door and turned fully to me.

"You still have not answered my question, mister."

"Actually, if memory serves me, you asked two questions."

She began to show signs of being annoyed so I knew I had to do a better job of drawing her interest.

"How I know you is extremely complicated and when the time is right I will gladly tell you. Your second question is not so difficult but who I am is not as important as what I do … not at this present time anyway."

She looks at her watch then crosses her arms and mentally decides to give me an ear.

"My name is Theodore Devlin and I represent a prestigious law firm whom I will not mention at this time. We have watched you for a few years now and we know talent when we see it. We only recruit the best and our success is based on yours. We are striving to become the most powerful organization on this planet. Our future looks good because we recruit young. We fashion, shape and mentor while the applicant is young and impressionable ... in most cases."

"So, you're some type of recruiter I gather?"

"Yes, as a matter of fact, that is exactly what I am."

"So what do you want from me? And how do you even know me?"

"You are Gabrielle Milos. Your professional name is Giselle Milian. You attend Notre Dame High School and you currently hold a 4.0 GPA. You belong to the Drama Club and you love aerobics. Some may even say you're a fanatic when it comes to aerobics. Your parents—well intentioned as they would like to think they are—are detached from reality; theirs and yours. They are completely oblivious to who their daughter is and what their daughter does. You plan on attending Rider University after graduation where you will major in economics ... a profession our law firm will be in need of in the future. You have no girlfriends you hang out with or even call. The boys at school believe you are either stuck up or perhaps a lesbian. As a matter of fact, you only see the male species as potential customers ... a means to an end. You have the ability to separate your personal life—ordinary and mundane as it is—from your professional life which, you find great joy in. You have never been arrested for anything ... not even a traffic ticket. So, as you have heard and should now clearly see ... we are very interested in recruiting someone like you. One who knows just how to do a little dirt and still manage to come out clean. You do know what I am referring to, don't you?"

It happened over a year ago. A friend of a friend of a relative of a customer had given Gabrielle a call to get together one evening. This person was supposedly the nephew of a customer who went by the name of Dr. Albert Demonde. Big Al, Gabrielle called him, not because he was your proverbial, "Big man," on campus or because he owned some humongous fortune 500 company. It wasn't even because he was some overweight,

gluttonous slob. It was because Al always dreamed big. Not like some punk drug dealer who wants control over a neighborhood but someone who envisioned owning an island or even a country. Albert was once the superintendant of a school for, "troubled boys," in Jamesburg, New Jersey. In this profession, Albert could mold these boys into the men they would become; the men he chose to mold them into.

So Al's nephew, Victor made the call to Gabrielle, told her who he was connected with and she said yes. The date would consist of dinner at the Hyatt's Garden Restaurant and later, room service of another kind.

Dinner went well, as expected. Both Gabrielle and her new friend Victor exchanged pleasantries and awaited their turn to be seated. Although both were still in high school, they appeared a lot older. Victor reminded her of a once, younger Big Al. Victor possessed those same big dreams as Albert and added that same touch of realism and possibility to them. Gabrielle found herself more forthcoming and open than the usual clients she catered to. It was all becoming more personal than she would ever allow a date to become. Dinner then lead to dessert, coffee and a little more conversation.

Because Victor did not appear in a rush to go to the room and handle the real business, Gabrielle let her guard down even more. Gabrielle actually started to become emotionally attracted to Victor.

The check came to the table and Victor slapped a platinum card inside the leather billfold without looking at the cost of dinner. The waiter took the billfold and returned the card to Victor. The two of them began to head to the elevator to the honor floor.

Victor and Gabrielle chatted and laughed like a couple who had known each other for some time. To onlookers, no one would have ever guessed that the two of them were on a first date.

They arrived at the hotel room and Victor used a fancy key card to unlock the door. Once inside, Victor sounded the word, "illuminate," and the lights turned on in the foyer and main room. This fascinated Gabrielle. She had no idea that such technology even existed.

She could only reply with, "How impressive. I have been to this hotel once or twice and didn't know they had rooms so technologically advanced."

Victor gave a short but quick, "Well, to tell you the truth, this is probably the only room in the entire place that comes with extraordinary amenities."

"I can hardly wait to see those other … extraordinary amenities," she sheepishly chuckled.

"I think you will find I'm full of delightful surprises. I always aim to please. But for now, why don't you go to the bathroom. I have a nice gift for you there. In the meantime, I'll fix a couple drinks and get comfortable myself."

Gabrielle walks through the living room which the hotel spared no expense to please any guest. The living room was complete with a wet bar at one end, a huge, cherry wood writing table with a computer, printer and fax machine at the other, and beautiful lamps and pictures accenting the tables.

The bathroom was a delightful sight—extremely roomy—equipped with a double-size tub complete with pearl and brass fixtures, a changing room, and plenty of counter space for the out-of-towner who almost always brought along more hygiene supplies than they would ever need.

There on the countertop lay an expensive-looking, long, black box with a gold ribbon securing the contents inside. Gabrielle sat on one of the two stools at the counter and carefully gave the box a little shake. "Some type of nightie," she guessed. She opened the box and looked inside—another pleasant surprise. She had all kinds of evening wear—the kind a woman wears when she entertains in the bedroom—but this was truly extravagant. It was a two-piece turquoise teddy with a sheer, topaz robe, reminiscent of something from another time and place.

She looked for a tag—something which would give her some idea as to how much Victor paid for one night of pleasure.

To her surprise, there were no tags indicating the designer or place of origin. She did know one thing—this garment was of a high quality silk—not even Victoria Secret could touch this item.

"I guess I would be expecting too much for this to fit me," she said in a low whisper. She put the two piece ensemble on and it fit perfectly; almost as if it were tailor made for her.

She exited the bathroom and entered the living room to the sound of, "Embrasse-Moi," by Les Nubian, playing at the right level where they

could speak to one another without shouting their dialogue and thereby, killing the mood.

Gabrielle asked Victor, "You have to tell me about this nightie? I saw no tags and I cannot guess where it came from."

"Aw, c'mon, take a stab in the dark about its origin."

"Well, if I had to guess, I would say Milan, Paris or some other part of France, but as for the timeline ... you got me."

"Well, you were right about France ... Bordeaux, to be exact. As for the timeline ... it's an original 16th century creation, well preserved through time."

"My goodness ... you're not serious are you? Something like this has to cost a fortune."

Gabrielle soon felt a little uncomfortable. She felt unworthy of something so ethereal. She began to pull away. Gently, Victor pulled her back to him.

"Look Gabrielle, I know what you do but that's not who you are. You have, I've been told, always been a confident young lady with great conviction.

Now, I know men have showered you with trinkets and tokens of ... appreciation for your services. But they have not the slightest clue about what a woman like you is really worth. My uncle claims you are a valuable commodity. You have yet to realize just how valuable you really are."

Gabrielle was speechless; frozen in place. No one has ever said such things to her. Most of her clients rushed the time pretending not to. This made her more uncomfortable to say the least.

Trying to swallow and gain some composure Gabrielle asked, "And just why am I so valuable? I've done nothing special with my life to this point. It is true; I have a few friends in places that will serve a future purpose for me. I even have a little money put away to further my education. But I don't see how that's valuable to anyone else."

"Like my uncle, I too, am a visionary. I see many possibilities in people—people who just require a little assistance and ... motivational training."

"And just what type of assistance and motivational training do I need?"

Victor handed her a drink and tapped his glass to hers. They drank.

"The type one usually receives against their will," he grinned.

"And just what is that suppose to mean?"

"Well, we sort of push people in a direction they would not generally go in."

Gabrielle tries to change the subject. "Are you really Dr. Demonde's nephew …? I see no real resemblance."

"No. I am one of the boys from the facility who call him uncle. I am one of those who were hand-picked … trained and fashioned for the cause."

"And what cause is that, may I ask?"

"I believe someone else more qualified should and will answer that. But for now, I think we should leave the business stuff for another time."

He gestures to her to finish her drink as he gulps the rest of his drink down. She follows his lead and finishes her drink when a thought came to her; a dreadful one. She realized she had, for the first time in her life, let her guard completely down. She allowed a non-bartender the privilege—and unchallenged trust—of making her a drink, without witnessing it. Without making sure it was safe to drink.

As she lowered the glass from her lips, Gabrielle was now in plain view of a smile she could no longer trust. A small stream of panic and trepidation began to nestle in the pit of her stomach. She had only one thought; to get out to the hallway, stick her fingers down her throat and regurgitate the contents therein.

But it was too late for that. She began to feel a little fuzzy. Her legs were getting weak as she grabbed Victor's arm to regain her now compromised, balance.

"What's the meaning of this?" she said to him.

Victor just smiled, snapped his fingers and two young men entered the hotel room. Victor panned her towards the door so she could view her new visitors.

The two young men were almost identical in every way—height, weight, skin tone and hairstyle and texture—not twins but definitely related.

Victor positioned himself directly behind her and whispered in her ear, "Allow me to introduce you to two very talented brothers … Anthony and Michael Porter."

Both brothers smiled and said nothing. Victor then pushed Gabrielle forward, just hard enough to land into the welcoming arms of Anthony and Michael. Victor then walked over to the three of them. He gently positioned his index finger and thumb on Gabrielle's chin, lifting her head so that they would be completely face-to face.

"Don't worry my dear; the drug I gave you will not knock you out. We prefer it more when our guest is conscience and aware of what's being done to them."

Gabrielle's reply to that was, "When this is over, I suggest you kill me. Because if you don't, I'm gonna wear your balls for earrings."

"My uncle was right about you … you're just as cool under pressure. The drugs will keep you calm. We will see how well you can collect yourself when this is over."

The three men take her to the bedroom and the door closes behind them to the sounds of laughter and revelry. All three of them have several turns with her; the smell of sweat, semen, and Gabrielle's perfume permeated the air. She could taste her own blood—slowly streaming from her nose—courtesy of a punch one of the young boys administered.

Victor walked over to the cabinet and changed the music to something more suitable for the mood—a heavy metal song from Tools Undertow album.

He then pulls out special tools from the cabinet including a whip, a very long dildo, and a leather and rubber strap he would use to gag her.

Victor returns to the bed, grabs Gabrielle by the hair and pulls her where they are nose to nose. "Hang in there, baby … the night is still young and we have so much more in store for you."

He pushes her head back while one of the boys repositions himself for his next turn. Gabrielle begins to send her thoughts to another time and place; on when and how she would one day return the favor to Victor. In spite of what was currently happening to her, she manages to smile at this thought.

CHAPTER 5

"You don't have to worry about your past, Ms. Milos. I'm not here to blackmail you. And from what I hear, your *friends* truly deserved their fate. I only wish I were there to see it. Tell me something, Ms. Milos … did you really make his genitals into a pair of earrings?"

Gabrielle looked me in the eyes. She did not blink; didn't even flinch.

"You do not have to answer that. It is probably for the best that I do not know something of such a … delicate nature. I guess what I am most curious about is to know whether or not you are a believer. For instance … are you a religious person?"

"I think you already know the answer to that since you claim to have been watching me for so long."

"I am a man of many talents but a mind reader, unfortunately, I am not. Besides, I would prefer to hear the words from your mouth if you please."

"I really don't know what this has to do with this … so called 'interview' but I'll bite. To tell you the truth, I have never given any of that much thought. I mean … what I'm trying to say is … I try not to concern myself with what others believe. Now, do I know right from wrong? Yes, I do. Do I believe in heaven and hell—Karma and the great reincarnation principle? I really don't have a clue about any of that. I guess what I'm really saying is … I believe in me and trust only me. Does that answer your question, Mr. Devlin?"

"I believe maybe you are the mind reader, Ms. Milos. You seem to have known what was next to come out of my mouth. You continue to impress me. And believe me when I tell you this; it is not easy to impress me. Anyway, I believe you would agree that this parking lot is hardly the suitable place for a formal interview. What do you say to that little outside café over there? I could buy you a coffee or lunch … whatever you prefer and, I will actually pay you today for just a little of your time. What say you, Ms. Milos?"

"And just what do you think my time is worth?"

I reach in my suit pocket and pull out a thin, white envelope and hand it to her. She turns the envelope so that it is right side up, revealing the name Giselle Milian, the name she uses to disguise her accounts as well as, her true identity. She begins to lift the unglued flap but stops and looks to me, as if to be granted approval.

"Like you said, Ms. Milos … you trust and believe in only you. Go ahead and take a look. It would take a lot more than that to offend me or my intentions."

Gabrielle reaches in and removes a check from the envelope. She studies the date, heading, her name—which was spelled correctly—and finally the amount. Gabrielle, once again, looks me in the eyes asking, "All this for an interview? I don't know what to make of this. Generosity to me always has a catch. And I have learned, long ago, to trust my instincts."

"That is exactly why we have decided to make a generous offer to recruit you. You are quite the meticulous sort whose thoroughness I find somewhat refreshing. Shall we?"

I raise my arm pointing in the direction of the outdoor café. She looks in the direction, looks to me again and nods her consent. We both walk over to the café.

The café contained all the pleasantness imagined. There were small, cozy round tables which comfortably seated two and more larger square tables for four or more. Black, iron tables with an ivy pattern from the top of the rim to its bottom—resembling the paws of an animal—like those found on an old-fashioned, cast iron tub. The top of the tables had black marble with white and grey swirled in and polished to a lustrous sheen. The chairs matched in color and resembled 17th century French royalty. A black and white canopy helped to shade the tables closest to the picture windows of the café while umbrellas—also black and white—provided shade to the tables on the sidewalk. The sidewalk itself was a smoke grey marble which also displayed an ivy pattern that snaked its way to the café. Each table came complete with a china set up and silverware. A single candle adorned the center of each table.

As Gabrielle and I walk along the grey marble floor of the café a waiter happily escorts us to a small table at the end of the sidewalk. We sit as the waiter quickly, but with grace and precision, flipped both coffee cups

with a tiny, 'tink,' and handed each of us a medium sized menu which also displayed ivy on its borders.

"Are you ready to order or shall I give you two a few minutes?"

"Tea for the lady ... lemon, one sugar and I will have coffee ... black, one sugar."

Gabrielle glanced over to me offering a slight nod of approval. The waiter acknowledges the order with a nod of his own and leaves.

"As I was stating earlier Ms. Milos, we could use someone like you for a job or two and hold you on contract for whenever we need your particular services in the future."

"And just what services would I be performing for your company? A call girl ... or maybe some sex slave for some perverted dignitary?"

"We prefer to call your job title, 'International Escort'. It is how you say, amiable in nature as well as on the surface. The truth is you are only to be used to create a distraction for the real job at hand."

"And just what job would that be? After all, if I am to create some distraction ... a sociable distraction, then I would like to know the degree of danger involved."

"I can assure you it would be at a bare minimum ... the danger that is. We will have many operatives watching your every move which is why you are only an escort ... nothing more."

"And you believe I would be suitable for this job? It sounds to me, that any call girl could perform this function ... someone more experienced, perhaps."

"It is true, we need a professional—someone with no real attachments—someone who has been in the trenches on an international level. We believe that someone could easily be you. With the proper training, you could prove to be one of the finest operatives at the firm."

"I cannot imagine why you believe this person is me ..."

"I find your lack of self-confidence quite surprising ... and disturbing. This attitude does not and has never suited you. So, let's put an end to it."

Gabrielle lifts her cup and slowly brings it to her lips. I lean back in my chair, cross my legs, and place both hands on my knee. Neither one of us speak. Gabrielle returns her cup to the dish and says nothing. More silence. The two of us become motionless until the waiter approaches. The waiter looks to me and then to Gabrielle. The waiter clears his throat.

"Ahem, are you ready to order or do you require a little more time?"

"We are ready … the lady will have the Caesar Salad, creamy Italian dressing on the side and I will have the Chicken Quesadillas, lightly grilled. Also, could you bring the lady a small dish of croutons on the side?"

"No problem, I will return shortly with your order," replies the waiter.

The waiter leaves and Gabrielle decides to break her silence.

"You know how I take my tea and you even know how I like my salad. What else do you know about me?"

"I know some days you like what you do and other days you wish you never met your aunt's fiancé. On the days you hate your occupation, I believe you think of him."

Gabrielle gives me a perplexed look wondering how I could possibly know this of her. She tries to recall if she ever—consciously or unconsciously—shared these feelings out loud. I then noticed her trying to process what I had just shared about her; I allow her a moment to assimilate.

"Shall I continue?"

"Sure … I can hardly wait to hear how much more about me you seem to already know."

"You love classical music but you have yet to meet a client who shares such exquisite taste in music. You are a big fan of the New York Philharmonic Orchestra but you rarely go. It makes you uncomfortable … the looks you get from patrons seeing you unaccompanied at such functions. It gives you some satisfaction when their men look at you wishing you were on their arms, instead of their wives."

Gabrielle begins to smile. "It serves them old hag's right. Some days they look at me with their disgust or pity … and sometimes, both."

"Except the one evening a prominent politician approached you and invited you to accompany him and his wife. You had that 'young look' about you that evening and could easily pass for his daughter or niece."

Gabrielle thinks back to that evening and how well-timed that gentleman had approached her. She was already feeling a little anxious and defensive in regards to the looks she had been receiving from the other patrons. Gabrielle found his actions extremely chivalrous. I continued.

"By the way, what did you do with the business card he slipped in your hand as he wished you a good night?"

Gabrielle looks to me more puzzled than ever.

How could he, know that, she thought.

The waiter returns with our meals, serving Gabrielle first.

"Enjoy your meal, sir … madam."

"Looks good … Here is a little piece of information I would like to share with you. That gentleman—the politician—is actually an employee of our firm. He was recruited by us before he graduated from Trenton State. He too, required some training and has been quite a success. Would you believe his humble roots began in an orphanage? His mother and father died in a car crash when he was about six. He had no relatives who would take him in. He was transferred from one family to another; quite the handful he was. But he was an ambitious young lad who only needed some guidance from someone … like I said, we recruit young."

"Maybe one day you could introduce me to him. I would like to personally thank him again for that evening a few years ago. I misplaced his card somewhere and never found it."

"I do believe that can be arranged. He will be running for Mayor in the next primaries.

If all goes well, he will be a shoe-in for that seat. And with our firm backing him, his opponent would have to make a deal with the devil to defeat him."

Gabrielle let out a little chuckle saying, "It sounds like someone else has already beaten him to the punch."

"Now that is the Gabrielle I like … perceptive and witty."

CHAPTER 6

Halfway through the meal I decided to change the conversation.

"Ms. Milos, do you believe there is a God and that there is a heaven?"

"I have never really given that subject much thought. My parents never talked about God, heaven, religion or anything related. They talked about bills, vacations, the neighborhood declining, and money—always money—stocks, bonds, shares, holdings, aggressive global investments … you name it."

"Well, that sure explains why you are so finance-minded. You probably have savings already close to six figures. That is, not including your recent consignment from us."

"This would put me over that mark, should I accept the offer," she remarks, touching her pocket where the check was placed.

Gabrielle reaches for a crouton on the dish when I gently and fatherly, place a hand on hers.

"Ms. Milos, I think you should know that not one of our recruits earn below seven figures. I believe that is something more for you to chew on."

I remove my hand, leaving her turning the crouton between her thumb and index finger.

That is something to chew on.

"Like I was saying, I have never had an opinion regarding religious doctrine. Besides, believing or even thinking about such matters in my line of work …"

"Would be too much for the heart and mind to bear," I sympathetically replied. "And I can only assume that it would be most difficult to do the work you do with a spiritual or even a moral … conscience?"

Gabrielle sets the crouton to rest on the dish and slowly pushes the dish towards the center of the table indicating she has had enough—with the meal, anyway.

"The reason I asked this particular question is to make sure I have a clear understanding of your thoughts in such a matter. I want to be

assured that when the moment of truth emerges you will not have a crisis of conscience. It would not bode very well to jump into a pool of water and then realize it is no longer your intention to get wet."

Gabrielle replies, "I think there is more to your question than my conscience and wondering whether or not I can accomplish a task set before me. And before this interview goes any further, maybe you should enlighten me on the significance of my beliefs … or the lack thereof."

As if pleased by Gabrielle's inquiry I merely smile.

"As you probably already know, happiness is only attained by those with real perception. Perception is vital for any real power. Power without perception is not real power at all—from the CEO of a fortune 500 company to the street level drug dealer—perception is a must … a necessary survival tool. Otherwise, the CEO goes bankrupt and the drug dealer gets imprisoned or killed. There is a place we all go when our time is up and it is not heaven. Sure, heaven does exist for some but for most of us—repentant or not—heaven is no longer a consideration. You and I stand a greater chance of winning a billion-dollar lottery than making it to heaven. The requirements are far too unrealistic to achieve yet, millions upon millions go through this life deluded, that if, they confess their wrongs they will get a pass to this place of so called 'solitude and effulgence'.

"And you know all this, how?" Gabrielle inquired. "Are you some kind of ex-priest, kicked out of some parish and this is now some vengeful attempt to get back at them?"

"I guess you could say that … part of it, anyway. You see, I have extensive knowledge of the Old and New Testament. I even have knowledge of several books that are no longer in print or never put into circulation. So, when I tell you these things it is not because of something someone else told me. Like you, I research thoroughly until I find what I'm looking for."

Gabrielle begins to respond but decides not to. She realizes that this is no ordinary subject for me; more deterministic and not at all, a sense of randomness.

"You see, there are 'Ten Commandments' from God and if you have broken even one, you are not allowed in. People believe … are deceived that as humans they are supposed to sin so they can ask forgiveness and all is well. My dear that is what I call 'having smoke blown up your butt'."

Gabrielle replies, "So, this is as close to heaven as anyone gets?"

"Oh, on the contrary, this is the only heaven most of us get. Every day, at least one person gets to go to heaven—the best out of all who die that same day—statistically speaking. If a plane full of priest's crash, only one will go. Now, children get an automatic pass. By the way ... priests make great slaves."

"Slaves ... what do you mean by that?"

"Well, it's like this. When a person dies, they either go to heaven or become a hell bound—a slave, foot soldier, enforcer or a guardian. There is a fifth position but only one can hold that ... title."

"And who holds that position?"

"That is the position of Commander or Master—Mr. Lucifer himself. Some positions are negotiable and promotable ... all with one exception. And that is the position of slave—once a slave, always and forever, a slave. They are also known as 'Helots'."

"Why haven't I ever been told this before? Not that it really matters but I have never heard anything about this on film, radio, television, or in person by anyone until now."

"This is not the kind of stuff the religionist types talk about. It is one of the many kept secrets to control and manipulate the masses. If this information were to be released to the world—with some proof provided—mass hysteria and chaos would emerge. The planet itself would be destroyed ... game over ... no overtime. Where would the fun in that be? No, it is far greater to let the two puppeteers play it out their way. Besides, this planet will serve a far greater purpose at the 'end of days'."

"This is so nuts ... I mean, it's difficult to digest," replied Gabrielle. "I mean, how could you know, any of this unless ..."

"I already hold one of those positions here ... on earth. Once again, your questions come as no surprise. The positions of Enforcer, Enforcer 1, and Guardian may serve in hell or on earth. You have probably walked past hundreds—no thousands of them. You see them on television and you hear them on the radio. They are everywhere and can be anyone."

"So which one are you ... an Enforcer ... a Guardian? And exactly what would be the job descriptions for those positions?"

"Well, to begin, hell does exist and there are many tongues for what hell represent. For instance, the Greek—my personal favorite—refer to hell as 'Hades', after the Greek god Hades. There are three levels of

Hades—Tartarus, being the place with fiery lakes and most offensive. This is the picture most people believe hell to be and they are not totally wrong about that. But the fact is hell has a limbo, as well as a glorious place. This is where Guardians—second in command, the Enforcer 1, and Enforcers move in and out of hell and earth. Every soul in hell works to make it to that glorious place—Elysium—but only a handful qualifies. Asphodel is Greek for Limbo—grassy fields and meadows—where a soul waits to see what position he will be granted. That is, unless you are already at the bottom of the pecking order ... a slave or helot. Those individuals are streamlined to Tartarus where they serve—and are tortured—forever. The Foot Soldier is below the Enforcers. Their job is to punish and torment the slaves."

"Can anyone be promoted ... I mean if you are a Foot Soldier or a Guardian can you be promoted?" Gabrielle inquired.

"All positions are promotion-capable except the slave. There are no known proclamations to set them free. Besides, slaves are composed mainly of pedophiles, gang members, drug dealers, and other low life's who lack any real significance, courage and creativity."

"You still have not answered the first part of my question. Which one are you?"

"Let's just say I have the ability to move from hell to earth. I do not molest children and I am no 'street-grease' drug dealer. That, I am afraid, is all I am allowed to tell you."

"Maybe hearing all this should encourage me to straighten my life out; go to church, become a believer, and go to heaven when I die. What do you think about that, Mr. Devlin?"

"What I think is not at all that important. What is important is, do you really believe you stand a chance at heaven or going to hell now, after what you did some time ago? You do know what I am referring to now don't you?"

CHAPTER 7

Victor Guerren walks into the Candlelight Lounge one evening to unwind after a long and tiring day of making deals. He finds a quiet spot in the back and orders a scotch and soda from the waitress. Patrons who know Victor pass by his table and pay their respects. Others from neighboring tables hold their glasses up in salute to him. Such salutations only go to perpetuate his feelings of being in charge and practically untouchable. After all, he did have a powerful uncle who no one would dare cross.

Then she walked in—tall and slender with mulatto features. Although Victor preferred the bronze skinned beauties, it was a delight from time to time to meet a lady not entirely brown of skin but not too pale either—so this lady was tailor made for him. She takes a seat at the bar and orders a white wine. The bartender pours it for her and as she begins to pay for the drink the bartender waves her off, telling her the drink is already paid for. Upon hearing that, she looks over her left shoulder to see Victor, already approaching her.

"I hope I did not offend you by picking up your tab, my dear but I felt it was one way I could come over and introduce myself. My name is …"

"Victor," the lady replied. "I have seen you before and I know your name. This is not that big a town and you are not what one sees as 'small change'."

"Do you have a name or should I just use my imagination?"

"And just what kind of name would your imagination come up with?"

Victor began to look her over. She had on a turquoise blazer with a black miniskirt, a belt which matched her blazer, princess cut diamond earrings which were large but not at all gaudy, a diamond heart necklace which helped to draw attention to her healthy cleavage, and a recently done French manicure which told him she was a woman of good taste and leisure. Expensive nude panty hose which accented her shapely legs and black, six inch heels—size eight, by the looks of them.

"If I were to guess, you must have a name that's profoundly pretty … something exotic … Amethyst … Jasmine … Salomé …"

She chuckles. "You're cute and those are nice names but I'm afraid you are wrong on all counts. My name is Cynthia … Cynthia Porter."

"Well, I think Cynthia is a lovely name … not plain or fancy … just right, I think. So Cynthia, what do you do for a living?"

"I'm into public service and relations. But I only work in the evenings if you know what I mean."

"I believe I know exactly what you mean. I guess I shouldn't be surprised but I sort of hoped …"

"You hoped I was the type you could take home to momma."

"Well, I have no momma but I do have an uncle."

"And what would Big Al say about me?"

Victor smiled, drained his glass and motioned to the bartender to hit him again.

"What do you say to one more drink and leaving this place?"

"You sure it's what you wanna do? People here know what I do."

"Well, lucky for you, I'm a sucker for green eyes."

They both smile, finish their drinks and leave. Unfortunately for Victor, he did not notice he was being watched … carefully.

CHAPTER 8

Victor and Cynthia pull up to a hotel on Lafayette Street and park. They walk inside and as Victor begins to go over to the front desk of the lobby Cynthia gestures to him that it was unnecessary; she already had a room reserved for them on the 'honor floor'. Victor chuckled at the idea of her having a room on that floor. The two of them proceed to the elevator and head to the thirteenth floor.

They come to the door which displays the number HON14. Cynthia turns the 'maid service required' tag around so it now reads 'Please do not disturb'. Once inside, Cynthia tells Victor to fix them drinks while she freshens up. Cynthia goes into the bathroom while Victor pours them both a scotch on the rocks.

Cynthia enters the room wearing an elegant black, lacy camisole and releases her hair so that it drapes the front of her shoulders, which gives her an even more, slender look to her five-foot, nine-inch frame.

Victor's only reply is, "And what exactly do I owe for the pleasure of all this?"

"If you have to ask, then you cannot afford me," Cynthia says with a casual smile.

Victor pulls out a knot of fifties that could choke a horse—and its mother—and says, "I really don't think that's a problem. I just hate being disappointed."

Cynthia gently nudges him so he is now flat on his back saying, "I really don't think that will be a problem either." She begins taking off his clothes, stopping him from helping her. Victor decides to put his head back and begins to relax.

All of a sudden, Victor begins to feel a tingle. It starts in his face and moves down to his arms and lower extremities. He attempts to get up and realizes he cannot. He looks to Cynthia and finds her smiling, sinister-like.

"What have you done to me?" Victor says in an accusatory whisper.

"Just a little Pavulon in your drink to paralyze your muscles ... it makes things a little easier, don't you agree?"

Victor strains to turn his attention to the table and notices Cynthia had not touched her drink. "What's this all about? Who sent you? Who do you work for?"

"I think my employer can answer that best."

The door unlocks and a woman enters. Victor did not recognize her at first until she speaks.

"Hello, Victor. How does it feel having *your* drink doped? Brings back memories, doesn't it?"

"Gabrielle?"

"So, I see you do remember my name. I told you that killing me would have been in your benefit. Maybe you should have taken that suggestion."

Cynthia puts her clothes back on, goes over to the dresser and picks up the wad of cash Victor had tossed there. She then turns to Victor and says, "Thanks, Vic. I hope to see you around but I sincerely doubt it. Unlike you, I do believe this lovely lady here finishes what she starts."

Cynthia smiles and winks at Gabrielle as she leaves the room.

Gabrielle goes to her bag and pulls out a specimen cup—half full of some clear solution—and opens a flat, plastic case containing a scalpel. She looks at Victor while showing him the instrument. "I promised you I would have your balls and I am a woman of my word."

Victor begins to plead to her but realizes he could no longer speak—not even a whisper. A look of sheer terror develops on his face.

"Now, hold still Victor. I promise you, you won't feel a thing."

She begins to cut and Victor tries to scream—his mouth wide open but nothing comes out. Pavulon is designed to relax muscles. It does nothing to numb pain—not even the nerves.

Gabrielle sarcastically says, "My dear, I guess you can feel that. I guess I'll have to take that last promise back. This is for sodomizing me."

She resumes cutting—blood spurting up in cadence to Victor's racing pulse—while tears stream down Victor's now grimacing face ...

A car beeps its horn and Gabrielle returns to the present. She looks around and has to compose herself while I, silently and patiently, allow her to do so.

The waiter approaches and asks if there is anything else he can get for us. I tell him no and ask for the check. The waiter goes into his apron pocket and produces the check, placing it on the table closest to me and begins clearing some of the plates and cups.

"I want to apologize for making you recollect such a terrible time in your life but it was quite necessary to support our discussion. How could you or anyone possibly expect to be forgiven for that?"

Gabrielle, still collecting herself, could do nothing but slowly nod in apprehensive agreement to what I had resurfaced to her consciousness.

"Ms. Milos, I tell you all this because I would hate to see you spend the rest of your life trying to make restitution for harm done. It would be time and effort spent in vain. There can be no forgiveness for murder—especially the joy you felt torturing Victor. Your path already lies before you. And that path is hell. Your only real decision now is ... what level and position of hell you are willing to work towards."

"What about rapist ... do they also go to hell?"

"Oh, you want to know what happened to Victor ... you sure you want to hear this?"

Gabrielle gives me a harrowing look, unsure whether or not she indeed, wanted to really know the fate of Victor.

"Victor is currently serving an eternity in Tartarus ... where he is constantly ravaged.

And because his 'blade' was removed—by you—and all that remains is the 'chalice', he now knows the true feeling of being violated. Does this news please you? Does it afford you some small comfort that your little handiwork will forever, be appreciated?"

"I don't know how I feel about that but I know one thing ... my nightmares of that evening continue still; and most times I hate myself for them. I blame myself for letting my guard down."

"Well, maybe just knowing Victor's fate will now be enough to finally put those nightmares to rest. I hate to cut this interview short but it is getting late and I have another appointment to conduct. What shall I tell my employer, Ms. Milos?"

"Count me in, Mr. Devlin."

CHAPTER 9

Gabrielle decides to join this new firm and in no time becomes an integral component in the firms' Public Service/Assistance Dept. She meticulously adapts to all the 'ins and outs'—the refined intricacies her job title entailed. In less than two years she had become one of the top five infiltrators in the business and the top female in her department. And just as I once assured her, she now earn seven figures, works with fewer clienteles, and rarely, does she have to take her clothes off. And as I also assured her, the 'Night Terrors' became few and far away. Her old contacts are now a thing of the past. She now answers to the contacts she is contracted for only. This gives her more time for herself; enjoying the things which please her.

One evening while preparing for a night at the Mann Music Center—Anne-Sophie Mutter will be performing a violin solo of, "Lalo," accompanied by the, "Symphonie Espagnole Op.21 with Deiji Ozawa, conducting—the thought alone appears to put Gabrielle in a pre-hypnotic trance, was interrupted by a pager message almost vibrating her pager off the top of her vanity.

"This, I really do not need tonight," she muttered rather loudly while leaning forward to pick up the pager. She checks the number, picks up her phone and calls. She follows a series of voice commands and code numbers which finally, connects her to the party who paged her.

"I hope this is a call just to say hello," Gabrielle said as pleasantly as she wanted to. What she really wanted to do was bark at the person for such a well-timed intrusion.

"Oh, on the contrary, my dear," I replied. "I would never dare interrupt your evening of classical entertainment. In fact, I thought I would do you a favor."

"Okay, now what is this favor you would like to do for me?"

"Well, I know you love the Arts and I also know you have the propensity of going it alone—too often, I think—so I thought you would enjoy the company of someone who has an appreciation for symphony as you do."

"Why does this sound like work, Teddy?" Gabrielle said with a hint of suspicion and small undercurrent of disgust.

"Okay, you got me. But it really isn't work at all. One of our lawyers from the New York office is in town for a few days.

He has no attachments nor does he want any ... a man strictly about the business and money. But he does love classical music so when I mentioned your going to the music center he nearly jumped three feet in the air. He insisted that I call you. He said he would do anything to accompany you there."

Somewhat flushed and flattered by hearing someone else interested in the arts and dying to accompany her, Gabrielle recovered enough to ask, "Well, for your sake he had better not be a talker. One word and I will remove myself from his company ... I mean it."

"Well, is it okay for him to introduce himself before you walk inside?"

"You know very well what I mean. When the lights go dim, so should he."

"You got it ... not a peep. Should I have him pick you up or will you meet him there?"

"Teddy ..."

"Okay, okay ... I will have him out front at 6:30 sharp. Have a wonderful night, my dear."

"We will see."

CHAPTER 10

Gabrielle enters the top floor of her apartment to the sound of her answering machine trailing off the end touches of a message from the firm. She walks past the machine, not bothering to play the entire message. *If it is that important, I can always be reached by my pager.*

She enters her bedroom—a cozy, yet tastefully resemblance of the southwest—complete with Native American paintings and handicrafts, exquisitely displayed throughout the room. Gabrielle was always fond of some of the sights she had seen while spending a summer in Oklahoma. She had even gone to a 'Rattlesnake Derby' in Mangum County.

She stood by a cherry wood settee with cream upholstery and began removing her clothes, checking for blood, soot, and anything else which would blemish the furniture or carpeting. With her clothes balled up in her arms she walks to the hallway closet and produces a large trash bag from a box on the floor, placing her clothes in it. She knew she would have to dispose of this evidence and very soon. But first, a hot bath and a call to Teddy, explaining how such a lovely evening turned into a fiery disaster.

An hour and a half later, Gabrielle found herself lying on the bed trying to replay the evening—collecting her thoughts hoping to form something coherent and believable; some cohesion—an explanation which connects all the dots.

Was this a contract hit? And if it was, was it the work of the firm? What about me? Was I too, the target or just in the wrong place at the wrong time? This is too coincidental—too ill-fated. That guy really wanted to kill me. The mere idea of it seemed to ... turn him on ... strange look in his eyes ... so grandiose and pestiferous.

These thoughts begin to create ambivalence in Gabrielle. She begins to slowly understand and even respect the hit man's attempt on her life. She also came to the realization that she was more than a mere escort. Although she has always felt as if she were more, she did not fully believe it until now. She picked up her phone and used the speed dial mode to quicken her call.

"Ms. Milos … Gabrielle, how was your evening?"

"Please do not pretend to not know the answer to that Teddy. I need some information and I would appreciate the truth … if you are capable of that."

Regrouping and using a more, somber tone, I replied, "Of course my dear … my apologies. How may I help you? Ask me anything … please speak freely."

"First of all, I believe this was more than a friend and colleague in town to relax and enjoy an evening of leisure. This was a hit … plain and simple. Secondly, this … Foot Soldier's appearance tells me this is the work of the firm. So my question is … was I part of the hit or was this all designed to test my ability to survive?"

"I have always admired your mind, Ms. Milos. Since the moment I knew of your existence, I saw in you greatness … admired by some and feared by others. To confirm your theories and to answer your question requires some … how do you say … finesse?"

"I would be happy with just the plain, old-fashion truth," retorted Gabrielle.

"The entire evening had been designed to have this friend preoccupied with you while other matters were handled … matters which exposed this friend as in fact, an enemy of the firm. Someone special would have to carry out the orders to terminate this threat.

You, on the other hand, were only expected to go to the show with your escort with him, returning to the hotel alone. We had not anticipated you actually having a … nightcap with this … traitor. In short, you were not supposed to even be there."

Gabrielle, slightly embarrassed, had not considered that part; that it was only supposed to be a night at the symphony. No drinks following it and certainly not a trip to Carson's hotel room. She continued to listen.

"Anyway, once we were informed of this change, we had to proceed, hoping you would come out on the other side, unscathed."

"Unscathed? You call that situation unscathed? That man really wanted to kill me!"

"But he didn't, so stop selling yourself short and calm down. I had every confidence that you would be able to handle things. Or, at least,

escape the whole ordeal with minimal damage and you did. Nothing could be done to spare you of the events on this particular evening."

Gabrielle sat silently, unsure of what she was thinking and what she wanted to say.

The latter part of this evening's conversation she found numbing but less surreal. She found that some of the things stated to her earlier held some truth to them. But those parts she was unsure of still bothered her.

"I realize this recent event is not at all in your area of expertise Gabrielle but I assure you, this was all extremely necessary. I also realize this brings no comfort to you either but the fact is, there may come another time when you may find yourself in a precarious situation. After all, this is the business we have all chosen."

Gabrielle realizes this conversation is not a play on words. She wants to believe that she was not the target and yet, cannot completely rule it out. "So, what's the next step, Teddy?"

"You are going to take a few days off and allow this all to settle down. Report to the firms' west office on Tuesday for a formal debriefing—post-traumatic treatment so to speak—and then we will determine what your next assignment will be and when it will be."

"Fine … I will see you on Tuesday then."

"I have to tell you Ms. Milos, you did an excellent job tonight. I think you need to know that. It was better than I had expected; the hand to hand combat, getting rid of the evidence by burning the hotel room … much more than I expected. You are some kind of a survivor."

Gabrielle says nothing more and hangs up. She looks to the window and notices flashes of light outside. The sound of rumbling in the distance follows the flash. *Another storm is coming. I have to find a way to survive this next one.*

CHAPTER 11

Tuesday morning comes and Gabrielle is headed to the west office. She finds herself still trying to fit all the pieces together.

Then it occurs to her that she was intentionally set up. *He wants me dead, but why? What can he gain by killing me? Is it something I know about him that he fears or is it something more personal? Something I did to him or someone close to him? There's something about that grin of his. I've seen it somewhere ... but where? It reminds me of someone ... someone from my past perhaps ... but who? That ... sinister ... grin ...*

Then she gets a flash; and another. The flashes come faster like some celebrity standing before a mob of paparazzi. *That grin belongs to ... Victor! Was Victor his nephew? Wasn't Victor adopted? That's the only way he could know about the murder. I was discreet. I was careful. I even killed the hooker I hired to lure Victor to the hotel room. He knows. He knows and now he wants me dead. I have to get away. I have to leave the country. I have to change my name one more time and never come back. I'll go to the bank, close out all accounts, and take off.*

She comes to a stop behind a gray SUV waiting for the red light to change. Through the intersection a large, Fed Ex truck is double-parked on the corner with its hazard lights blinking. The driver exits the truck with two boxes and goes into the New Jersey National Bank. The light turns green and Gabrielle slowly follows the SUV through the light. The SUV begins to creep around the Fed Ex truck but has to stop, allowing oncoming vehicles to maneuver around the truck and come through the light. Gabrielle finds herself stuck in the middle of the street as she glances up to see the light is still green.

"C'mon, c'mon, hurry up you jerk. How many cars are you gonna let through? Edge out a little more," Gabrielle says under her breath.

Gabrielle hears an engine roaring from her left. She turns to see a truck grill in her driver's window. The truck hits her with a force so hard it pushes her car, flipping it through the intersection. Gabrielle feels a quick flash of

pain as her car is rolled over two times, leaving her upside down—facing north now instead of east. She wants to unbuckle her seatbelt but cannot move her arms. The air bag begins losing some of its fullness but it still blocks her view. Gabrielle begins to panic as she begins to smell gasoline and tastes her own blood. She tries to call out but only manages a raspy, whisper. She panics even more when she realizes she can no longer feel her legs. She hears footsteps coming from the rear of the vehicle. The footsteps are getting closer now—shoes crunching on glass. She shifts her eyes to a figure kneeling down on all fours. A hand moves the air bag enough allowing his head to peer in at her. The person begins to speak and she recognizes it as my voice.

"Like I said, I have always admired your mind. I knew—sooner or later—that you would figure most of it out."

"Teddy?" Gabrielle said in a low, raspy tone.

"Careful, my dear—you seemed to have suffered quite a bit of damage to your spine and vocal cords. I am amazed you can talk at all ... a side impact of this magnitude usually snaps the driver's neck. Lucky for you, you turned just in time."

"So what happens now, Teddy?" Gabrielle grunted lowly.

"Well, let's see ... first, your lungs will continue to fill with fluid making it impossible for you to breathe. Eventually, you will choke on your own blood ... a little more painful than I originally planned of course."

"But why this ... Was Victor your real nephew? He deserved what he got."

"A nephew of my creation and yes, Victor deserved what he got. Victor was scum but Victor was my kind of scum. When you killed him, you ruined my plans for recruiting a special prospect I have had my eyes on for some time. I really hate when people ruin my plans. Anyway, I guess I can now answer your question as to the position I hold."

"No need," Gabrielle gurgled, blood trickling from the corner of her mouth. "I already know ... now."

"I do like your mind. You are going to make an excellent Foot Soldier. And who knows ... you may even get promoted to Enforcer one millennia. By the way, I think you will really get a kick out of the torture I have prepared for you. It is to die for."

I then reach past Gabrielle and grabbed her handbag. I begin to rifle through it, pulling things out and flinging them all about the car. I find a plastic card and small key.

"Ah, here it is."

I look on Gabrielle one final time and smile. "I'll see you in hell, my dear."

CHAPTER 12

Later, that morning I stroll into the Yardville National Bank on South Broad Street. After a brief conversation with the bank manager and proof of Identifications, he escorts me to the back where all the safety deposit boxes are stationed.

I approach the box with the numbers 8-1-3. I take out the key from my vest and insert it into the keyhole. I look back to the manager who simply nods as he exits the room. Once I pull the box free of its cradle, I place the box on the nearby table. Lifting the lid to view its contents I can only offer my trademark grin. The box contained:

- $500,000.00 in cash
- $300,000.00 in bonds and stock certificates
- Assorted jewelry and precious uncut stones
- A photograph of her parents
- A clear specimen cup containing the entire genitalia in a clear solution.

I place everything in my satchel except the specimen cup. I hold the cup up to the light, still smiling. "I do admire that girl's mind. If I were the caring type, I would feel bad about Victor's dying that way. But I needed Gabrielle more. Besides, there was no other way to truly bring out a convincing evil—evil even she would truly believe to be … Unforgiving."

Epilogue: A note from Theodore Devlin

Who said, "Good help is so hard to find?" I hire all who are willing— especially and preferably those who are not. I have wanted Gabrielle since she was a child. And I placed people in her life to make our meeting possible; from her aunt's pedophile fiancé, to Carson Harding, Attorney at law. She will make a fine Enforcer with the power of sublimity—to pierce

another's consciousness with seductive cunning and precision, she will push many to join the cause with just a whisper. And it just so happens, I have an IT geek whose expertise I will need at a future time. But first, she must be punished for her apprehension and attempted betrayal. Gabrielle will be slowly eaten by wild dogs—recurring over and over again. Not only will she witness them tearing away at her entrails, she will feel ever bit of it. After a couple years of that, she will comply to anything I need her to do with not as much as a dirty look. She will become obsequious and supplicate—to me only.

This is far from over. There is still much work to be done. Like chess, I must anticipate His next move to remain in control of the field. Next stop—one who was born to serve me—a true killer.

"Let death seize them;
Let them go down alive into hell,
For wickedness is in their dwellings
And among them."

PSALM 55:15

CHAPTER 1

I met Russ, "The Grappler," Jericho at a prison in Jersey. Russ can only be described as the most antisocial of all sociopaths. He received his nickname at an early age. His first pet—a hamster named Carmel—he took great pleasure in choking to death because the hamster bit his finger while he was trying to feed it a sunflower seed. This was the first indicator that something was terribly wrong with Russ. Russ became fascinated with the blank stare of the dead. Professionals equate his mental maladjustment to synapses in his sadistic head that began to fire at his first taste of death and has not stopped firing since Carmel.

Russ graduated from small rodents to kittens, puppies, cats, and dogs. He once antagonized a 150 pound Rottweiler named, 'Roscoe'. Russ only outweighed that animal by twenty-five pounds, so the advantage belonged to Roscoe who possessed a bite strength that could take a child's head clean off its body. But knowing this only added to Russ' excitement. Armed with nothing but a pair of batting gloves, he took Roscoe head on. When it was over, poor Roscoe laid prostrate on the ground—tongue hanging out of his mouth—with that blank stare. Russ would spend hours in a prone position looking at that blank stare; a smile on his face humming to the tune of Queens', "Another one bites the dust."

Russ moved on years later to strong armed robbery and eventually, murder. It wasn't the robbing that excited him but the ability to subdue his victim; the sound of his victim choking and fighting for their lives, created a ripple in Russ. From the top of his head to the tips of his toes, this gave him the power and satisfaction he lived for.

For Russ, this was far better than any sexual orgasm he would ever experience. Russ did not fair well with the ladies. He was just too antisocial and scary to engage, let alone, sustain a relationship with others on any level. As a result of his disposition, most women found Russ to be a little creepy.

Needless to say, this behavior went on for about a year and a half until he was caught in the act with victim number thirteen. Mind you, only one of the thirteen victims were female; his first victim. Russ found little pleasure and an even lesser challenge in overpowering the opposite sex. To Russ, it was less of a challenge than good ole' Roscoe. Besides, he pitied women being female and all. In his mind, women already had enough strikes against them. No, he preferred men. Not the 'metro' sexual male whom Russ thought of them as dazed and confused but the typical gangster-biker-thug-woman-abusing type of man. For Russ, these men were the equivalent of grade "A" heroin for the junkie.

CHAPTER 2

Prison did little to nothing to curb his appetite for inflicting pain on others. Russ had been placed in Administrative Segregation or what we call the 'hole', so many times that finally, the prison officials assigned him there permanently.

There, Russ would be visited by doctors, court appointed lawyers, (which he and most convicts hate and consider useless) psychologists, and priests. Not one cared to re-visit Russ after an initial session.

One psychologist gave up the profession after being severely choked by Russ. The final analysis on Russ' chart was summed up in one word: 'Incorrigible'.

One day Russ received a visit from me; this story, I am the warden of the prison. Warden Stuart Arthur Tannenbaum—a tall, slender man who wore old suits indicating that I was either frugal with my money or cared little for societies' view on fashion. I disguised myself with icy-blue eyes, hiding my actual age. Although I am clearly a man in my late sixties or early seventies, I chose to have the eyes of a young man who could probably 'scrap'.

Russ was sitting on his bunk when I entered his cell. Russ thought to himself, *either this man has a death wish or like me, has never met a man he couldn't lick.*

"What, no handcuffs for me before you come in? You're takin' one hell of a chance walkin' in here alone."

I then flashed a partial grin but said nothing as I dragged a metal chair, noisily inside the cell, stopped about three feet from Russ and sat. Russ could feel that jolt of electricity beginning to build inside his head; I too, could feel it. It had been some time since he had this feeling.

"Don't you think it would be wise for you to at least have three or four guards on standby? I'm not what you would classify a gracious host."

I looked at him expressionless which began to irritate Russ.

"I don't know what you're here for and I really don't care but you'd better open that hole of yours and say something because I don't care for you 'silent-probe-my-thoughts' type of people around me."

I continued with the silence which began to confound and infuriate Russ. He could deal with and understand his anger; confusion is what unbalanced him to no end.

"Russell Samuel Jericho, alias 'the Grappler', Born June 13, 1969 … the son of a deacon who did his best to keep you in the good graces of the lord …"

Russ' hands clench into fists; eyes begin to narrow, he stood but I motioned to him to remain seated.

"Please, allow me to finish and if you wish it, you can attempt to attack me." Russ sat back down. "Your mother died when you were only a child. There are no other significant others in your life. You are a recluse … a scourge on society. You could not adjust out there, so you are going to be our guest here … for awhile."

"I liked it better when you just sat and stared at me."

"May I continue, Mr. Jericho?"

"Sure, if you don't mind my laying down and ignoring the hell out of you."

"Your thirteenth victim lived and testified against you. As a result, you were sentenced to one hundred and fifty-three years on twelve counts of robbery and murder; no parole. That means you still owe me one hundred and fifty-one years. And I intend to collect each and every one of them."

I get up and begin to leave the cell. I turn to Russ, smile and raise my right hand flashing my fingers in the sequence, one-five-one. I turn away to exit as Russ yells out, "Fuck off and good luck getting that from me!"

CHAPTER 3

A few weeks later I return to find Russ pacing in his little 6' by 9' cell. This time I enter—minus the metal chair—with a scroll in my hands. Russ looks down and eyes the scroll.

"Whatcha got there warden, my parole papers?"

"I doubt you've ever been the type to use sarcasm. I am here because I need to ask you a couple questions. The first question is … do you believe in heaven and hell?"

Russ stopped pacing, stood straight with his arms crossed.

"To tell you the truth, I never gave either much thought. My father did all he could to cram that bible down my throat. He preached and thumped and testified until his voice damn-near gave out. That shit gave me a headache … every time. Finally, I choked him until he passed out. I left home and never saw him again."

"Why didn't you kill him? Victims passing out never stopped you before?"

"Because even with my hands around his throat … even with the veins popping out the sides of his temple … even though his mouth gasped for air, his eyes told a different story. Those eyes were too peaceful … soft, brown, and innocent. No fear of what was to become … no dread or foreboding. It was as if those eyes were expecting it."

I smiled lightly. "You did not feel that charge, did you? That charge you always felt with all the others was missing, right? You couldn't kill him because he wouldn't behave …"

"Like the others," replied Russ. "Killing him would not …"

"Curb your thirst … your hunger."

"Yea, something like that … if I don't feel it, then why even do it."

"What about now?"

"What about now, what?"

"Heaven and hell … have you given it any thought since your confinement?"

"Why, so I can sit in this shit-hole, feel sorry for myself and brood over the lives I've taken? That's what you people in charge want, isn't it? Well, that's not gonna happen. I won't give you screws the satisfaction of seeing me on my belly. I don't regret what I did and, if I had the chance, I would complete victim number thirteen and on, and on, and on …"

"That leads me to question number two. What would you say if I told you I am here to grant you a wish … another opportunity?"

"I would probably say something like … you're full of shit and there's no way humanly possible that you could grant me anything I need or that I could use."

I flash a bigger smile and gently pat the scroll in my lap repeatedly.

"Whether you believe it or not, an opportunity is exactly what I would like to offer you."

"So, are you gonna tell me what this is about or are you gonna continue to blow smoke up my ass."

"I'm here to help you but first, you will listen to what I have to say. You will find this hard to fathom in that thing you call a brain but give it a try anyway."

Russ places his back to the wall and shoves his thumbs in his waist band. "I'm all ears."

"First of all, both, heaven and hell exists. Those religionists did get that much right. But their views on everlasting life are both dogmatic and unrealistic. They have spent centuries deceiving humans … humans like your father. All the good he thought he brought to this world and still, did not qualify for heaven. That's right … he is in hell and you know something? He suffers like you would not believe. Your father suffers because he felt cheated and rightly so. After all, he was a pillar in his community. He contributed to charities and fundraisers. He never missed church and boy, oh boy, did he worship. His only problem was he couldn't quite get his head to match what was in his heart. You see, in his head, he thought God should have been able to reach out and touch you— God never came—your father couldn't understand why. Therefore, you became the sole reason your father did not qualify for heaven. You see, the resentment your father harbored in his mind slowly trickled down into his heart. This resentment was subtle … stealthy … and so far below his radar, that its predictability became … unpredictable. By the time your

father's number was called, he realized all too late that he had failed … himself and God."

"So my father paid the ultimate price for what … trying to keep me from paying it? Even if I believed you … even if I believed this whole afterlife concept, why would I believe my father—of all people—would crap out? It makes no sense to me. He'd never done anyone or anything harm. He only …"

"He betrayed the One who really matters. Your father carried Christ in his heart … side by side with Judas Iscariot. And by the way, Catholics are wrong about suicide. Suicide by selfish means will jet line you straight to hell. Suicide with purpose—killing you so many will live—is most noble. Judas did not go to hell for the suicide; he went to hell for accepting that cursed thirty pieces of silver. His greed lead to madness and his madness lead to suicide. So the big question still remains … how does one get into this place called heaven? Some believe in natural selection … the concept which led to the demise of the dinosaur. Me, I believe in pre-selection; establishing a bias for someone at birth and surrounding that person with hedges like God did JOB from the Bible … minus the contest, of course. At birth, a person is fashioned, molded, and manipulated I might add, and the rest must fend for them in vain, I might add again. Those who claim to fall from His grace and are born again is a farce; a fairytale we convince ourselves of so we can sleep at night. It is an illusion we tell ourselves so we don't run through the streets screaming like someone mad. I guess it is safe to say that you can now remove those blinders and deal with the truth. And the truth is this: You, Mr. Jericho are already condemned to hell. The second and equally important question is at what position in hell, will you qualify for?"

Russ began to deflate as if taking all this information in popped something in him, thereby, offering him some relief. The tightness in his jaw was gone. His fists were no longer clenched. It was almost as if, he had resigned himself to an inevitable fate.

"Okay, if what you say is true, then what is it, exactly that you want from me and what positions are you talking about?"

"The positions I am referring to are very similar to the levels of any big organization like the armed forces. You have a Commander-in-chief, generals, colonels, sergeants, and of course, the grunts. In hell's army there

are Guardians, Enforcers, Foot Soldiers and finally, slaves. All of these positions can be attained except, of course, Commander which we call Master. That position is for one and he will serve that position forever. Most of the other positions carry with them, certain benefits which you can learn of at a later date. We have millions upon millions of slaves. Your father is one of them. He can never be promoted. His kind suffers the most unimaginable, of all tortures."

"Why are you telling me this about my father? Why do you think I want or need to hear this? I could care less for that ... sperm donor."

"That is all I needed to hear, Russ. There can be no confusion about what you are and what you will be involved in. The afterlife holds no forgiveness; by Him or by the other. So now, we come down to it. You ask what this is I hold in my hand? You could say it is a type of release ... with a catch. I can and will release you but only on one condition. Do what I demand and I will set you free from this prison ... for good.

Fail me, and I will return you to this cell and from time to time subject you to a torture which will have you begging for the mercy of a quick death. Either way, I will find some enjoyment in either choice."

"And what is this demand you need from me, Mr. Warden? I hope it is something that I will enjoy doing."

"I need you to kill someone for me."

I hand Russ the scroll and back away.

"The instructions are enclosed. All you will need shall be provided to you."

Russ had to control what he was feeling and began reading the scroll. As I exit the cell I look back one more time to see Russ looking somewhat puzzled.

"If you decide to fulfill this task, then stand at your cell door this evening at 8pm. Say out loud, 'Thy will be done', and you will be set free. No one will try to stop you. Do all the letter commands and you will be rewarded."

I walk out; the cell door closes and locks with Russ still standing by the back wall—scroll open—hoping this is not some stupid game a warden plays with inmates.

If this is some joke, I will do what I wanted to the first time the warden came in here. I will experience that feeling ... that pleasure again ... one way or the other I will.

CHAPTER 4

It is now 8pm. Russ stands from his bunk and walks to his cell door. He holds the parchment in his left hand. He presses his right hand on the cell door and peeks out through the small window. He then yells out, "Thy will be done." The cell door unlocks and opens. Russ stands there at first then takes two steps forward and out of his cell.

This has got to be some kind of a twisted, friggin' joke. Any minute now, the screws will come out and beat the hell out of me. Then, after I come out of the infirmary, they'll charge me with attempting to escape—adding another five to ten years to my sentence. But even that won't really matter … it's not like I would ever get out anyway.

Russ begins walking down a corridor and around the corner, to a set of steps which lead down to another hallway. It is quiet; almost eerie. Two stencil-painted directions are on a blank, eggshell white wall. They read: Laundry (arrow points left) and Dining room (arrow point's right). He stops and unrolls the parchment. It instructs him to go to the dining room, through the kitchen to the loading docks. As he enters the dining room he stops in his tracks to the shock of seeing two guards at a table on the nearside of the room. The guards look up first at him, then at each other. Russ stands still and finds difficulty knowing what to do next. One guard stands, looks over to him and nods his head directing Russ to head in the direction of the kitchen. The other guard holds his coffee cup as if to say 'cheers' or 'congratulations'. Russ acknowledges the gesture with a nod of his own and makes his way to the kitchen.

Russ moves through the kitchen and spots the exit door. It is unlocked. He goes out the door and onto the loading dock. He pans around and spots a car idling in the lot. There is no one inside the car. He reads from the scroll again. It reads: *A car will be available to you. Just get in and drive about 2.7 miles. There will be a small rest stop there. A bag on the back seat will have a change of clothes, identification, and cash. Although it is not your style, be cool when you go in to change. No one will be looking for you. Change*

clothes, trash the prison khakis and get out of there. From there you will follow the directions to the motel.

Russ pulls up to the Sleepy Hollow Motel out on route one at about 8:40. He parks and goes to the office. A small man of Middle Eastern descent comes from the back room, looks Russ over and heads to the key rack. The clerk places a key on the front desk, nods to Russ and returns to the back room. He returns to the car and moves it in a more discreet section of the motel, which happens to be close to his room. He gets out and carries a couple bags to the room. He finds the room and double-checks the key. *Number 13 ... I didn't know that number was ever used ... it's suppose to be taboo; like being on the 13th floor somewhere.*

It is now 2 a.m. and Russ is still awake, lying on his bed, looking up at the ceiling. It is quiet except for the occasional sound of a tractor trailer roaring past on the highway outside. He begins hearing a small beep. He sits up and looks around the dark room. The beep continues as he gets out of bed, turns on the lamp, and attempts to pinpoint where the sound is coming from. He opens the top left drawer of the dresser and discovers a pager taped to a videocassette. He pulls both items out and spots a note attached to the cassette instructing him to 'play me'. He turns the television on, changes the channel from the porn station, adjusts the volume, and places the cassette into the VCR. It was a pre-recording.

"Hello Russ, I had a feeling you might still be awake. I certainly hope I am not interrupting anything. Then again—knowing you—you were probably just lying there, thinking. Anyway, I have to cut your vacation short so we can get down to business. In 24 hours one of our agents will lure a special guest to a hotel room where the agent will commence to make him as comfortable as possible. And at that moment—face to face—you should be coming for him. I don't have to tell you what I want done, now do I?"

"Well, I didn't think you freed me to take pictures and frame anyone. But why free me to do this? Couldn't he have just hired a professional?"

"In case you are wondering about this, I simply need someone who has a special talent—a propensity to kill with no remorse. You see, when that moment of truth arises, you will not fail me. You will have to quiet that voice in your head. You will have no choice but to feed that craving of yours. You will finally get victim number thirteen."

"And the agent who's supposed to lure this person to the hotel … is it safe to assume it's a she or is our guest one of those fruity-loop types; that will make killing him less sweet than I would like."

"Also, in case you are wondering, the agent is a she and you can even have her as … a bonus. Just think, it will be the first time you ever killed two in one shot."

"How can he anticipate my questions like this?"

"I do not want you to worry about that right now. I am a man of my word. Your success at killing was always natural … no reward … no special privileges … not for hire. And that is probably why you remained sharp … calculating … methodical. Remove the thought of recompense from your mind. It will only cause you to become careless."

After giving it some thought, Russ realized the warden was right. Russ agreed his mind must be sharp for this task. Going after one victim is normative for him so this time he will have to be quicker; much stronger; more adaptable. He cannot afford to be careless like he was the last time. He had underestimated his prey the last time out. He had not planned his attack like he had with the others. This attack was a 'spur-of-the-moment' moment. His attack was impulsive.

CHAPTER 5

The man yelled and disrespected the grocery store clerk—a frail and timid-looking young girl—probably still in high school. This verbal assault irritated Russ. For some reason, he had always pitied women for being the weaker sex. He had that taste in his mouth; that bittersweet taste he always had just before he attacked.

Russ paid for his items and hurried out behind the rude man. Keeping a safe distance, he followed the man across the street and around the corner. *This is perfect. This guy lives in the neighborhood. His guard will be down a little so when I make my move he will have to summon his adrenaline for survival.* The taste in his mouth grew stronger at this thought. As Russ continued to follow the man he began putting on his batting gloves and felt that familiar shiver down his spine. How he loved that feeling. He always visualized a fiery red streak down his back; like the way the hair on an animal's back rises when it becomes aggressive. He also imagined his eyes becoming dilated.

Russ intentionally stepped on a soda can to alert the man he was being followed. The man looked back and saw Russ. Russ had that menacing grin on his face which always raised concern with his victims. The man's pace became unsteady as he constantly panned his head to the left, over his shoulder to track Russ' pace. Russ maintained the same speed and direction toward the man. Russ never cared much for stealth. He always wanted his victim to see him coming. Russ could smell the fear on them like musk. But this time the smell wasn't there. Even with the toughest of opponents, he could smell it. This time the smell was absent. *This cannot be right.* Russ needed that smell. It made him stronger; more determined.

The man stopped and turned to face Russ. He no longer questioned the intentions of Russ—he knew what Russ wanted. Seeing the expression on Russ' face told the man that there will be no deliberation, no bargain talks, and no compromise. Like two samurai warriors, the two of them stood about ten or twelve paces apart. The man placed his bag at his feet

and took two paces forward. This move did not go unnoticed by Russ. It came as shock and surprise. Russ no longer needed that smell. He had discovered something else; confidence; confidence in his opponent; confidence without borders. *This man is clearly not like the others. He is more like me … probably used to irritating others into a fight … an instigator … now I really want him. I will take my time with this one … make him beg before I rip the life from him. Now I smell him … he is beginning to realize that I am not like the others … probably thinking too much now …*

So the contest began. Both men fought with incredible fury—the fury of a cruiserweight title fight—exchanging blows, blocks, and parries. But in the end Russ began to gain the advantage. After all, Russ lived for this. It was the only time he could see his purpose; feel control and find focus. Still, it took a few minutes too long to subdue victim number thirteen as a patrol car, early on its route, intervened and arrested Russ as he attempted to fully, strangle his victim.

CHAPTER 6

After giving his last attack some thought, Russ realized he had to have his wits about him this time. Time and timing—a careful sense—prudence. He always possessed this when engaging the enemy in this line of work. Russ knows he has to be quicker this time. *I hate not being able to take my time with this. I prefer to play a little with my prey but there's too much at stake this time. If I succeed, I am free.* Russ went to the kitchen of his motel room and pulled a V-8 from the fridge. He poured it is a glass and dumped half a bottle of Tabasco Sauce to top it off. He was fond of Bloody Marys but always drank them, minus the vodka. After guzzling half the glass, he grinned thinking how ironic it was to call it a 'Virgin Bloody Mary'. He turned off the television, turned the radio on low, and began planning his next move. He said aloud, "Let's hear you talk to me through the radio, warden."

CHAPTER 7

It's a cool Saturday night in Princeton. It's also a noisy one at the Best Western. Outside cars, trucks, and buses go whizzing by to destinations unknown and unimportant.

Some out-of-state college is celebrating a last second buzzer-beater victory over the home team. They will stay overnight and take off to Massachusetts in the morning. But for now, they are content to yell, scream, whoop, and holler the night away.

A shiny, red Cadillac pulls up and parks out front. Two figures exit the vehicle, nicely dressed as if they just left the theatre or some special function. The man takes the woman's hand and closes the passenger door. Arm in arm, the man and woman proceed to the hotel's front entrance. He whispers something to her and with a sly smile she replies, "I guess you're gonna have to wait until I get you in that room, now aren't you?"

The semi-anxious couple approach the front desk where the manager walks up and personally takes care of them. After a brief exchange of words and smiles, the key cards are handed to the man who thanks the manager and shakes his hand. In parting, the manager says, "Enjoy your stay and if you need anything, I will be here all night." The couple leaves the manager smiling.

Russ is already at that same motel. He has the curtains drawn, the radio on low—the music barely audible—and he is drinking another Bloody Mary; virgin. He is still listening to nothing except his own breathing which is getting heavy. He tells himself he needs to slow his breathing down. *How will you hear them enter the room with you sounding like some asthmatic dragon, Bud? Calm down and try to breathe easier ... easier ... yes ... that's it. It won't be long now.*

He hears voices outside coming closer. Russ begins to close his eyes to prepare for that rush he always gets before he strikes. He felt nothing— absolutely nothing at all. The sounds become clear now. It's two of the young men who were with the football team; not the targets.

He opens his eyes again to peer through the curtains. The balcony's overhead lights are bright. One of the lights just happens to be directly in front of the window next door. Russ hopes that light will not work against him when the time comes. *Maybe I can sneak out real quick and put it out.* He begins to go to the door when he felt the hair on the back of his neck stand up. He turned toward the window and froze. That rush was slowly beginning to form in his head, starting at the temples. But why; he had not heard anything. He closes his eyes and the sounds become clear now. Sounds of shoes coming his way—sounds of voices becoming clearer. It was his targets this time. There would be no mistaken the feeling he gets and is now getting. He knew in his heart the time had finally come. Soon, he will be getting his 'fix'. He will wait for them to get a little comfortable and 'the grappler' will pay them a visit.

CHAPTER 8

The sun has set for more than an hour and there is a clear, gibbous moon above the earth, casting both, light and shadow to all in its path. It's a beautiful night for romance; a brazen evening for a killing … or two.

Inside the motel room a prominent lawyer and his company—an escort who has done well flying below the radar and being completely discreet—are preparing to consummate their lovely evening. The room was finely accessorized with rose petals and scented candles. Mellow music played lowly in the background which, only further perpetuated the ambience. The lawyer is lying on the bed, wearing green silk boxers and nothing more. He is getting anxious waiting for his guest to exit the bathroom.

"Gabrielle, what are you doing in there? Don't make me wait all night." He leans over to the nightstand and lifts his glass of champagne just as his guest enters the bedroom. She is wearing a silver and white teddy, with just a touch of lace; truly an exquisite but erotic sight to behold.

"Are you ready for that surprise, counselor?"

The lawyer, mesmerized by this sight turns his glass up and in less than two seconds, empties his glass. His only response to her question is, "I have been waiting for this surprise since we said hello."

She climbs on the bed like a cat sneaking up on its prey with eyes fixed on its target. He pulls her to him, giving her a gentle kiss on her right shoulder. They begin to kiss when there is a small, unassuming knock on the door.

The two of them stop, turn towards the door, then back to each other. Another knock on the door and the lawyer looks to his guest with a slight grin. "I guess that's the big surprise on the other side of the door." She mistakenly thinks the surprise on the other side of the door is a gift from him to her so she smiles back.

The lawyer gets up and goes to the door. He removes the top latch, looks back at his guest and smiles again. He turns the knob …

There is a loud explosion as Russ bursts through the door. The force of his entry sends the lawyer hurdling through the air, on the bed and over to the other side with only the wall stopping his flight. In a flash, Russ is on top of the lawyer, both hands around his neck, pulling him off the floor. She can only watch in shock and horror as the assailant throws the lawyer onto the dresser, knocking over two of the many lit candles, the lawyers watch, and his pager. The lawyer tries to stop his ricocheting progress by attempting to use the television to regain his balance and composure. This is a feeble attempt as he and the television come crashing to the floor. The lawyer is trying to sort out what is happening. Just as he begins to realize he is under attack, Russ is on him, once again.

The lawyer looks up to see a fist coming his way. The fist finds its target, landing squarely on the lawyers left cheek. More punches follow in a blinding barrage of fury. Russ is clearly enjoying this. His victim is now in a helpless panic, trying to plead to his assailant to stop. This makes Russ enjoy it all the more. The lawyer tries to claw at Russ' face as Russ begins to place both hands around the lawyer's neck once more. He pans over to the bed to see what target number two is doing. He spots her running to the bathroom. Russ knows he has time now. Time to kill his prey in the manner he is accustomed to. *Good, after I'm done with this guy, I'll knock another door in and collect my bonus.*

The lawyer—still clawing, kicking, and flailing about—is now in an even greater panic. He knows there will be no litigating or negotiating with his attacker. No money will buy his way out of this. The lawyer looks Russ square in the eyes. He realizes his attacker is actually enjoying this.

Russ begins to grin harder as the gurgling sounds of his prey begin to dwindle. The eyes of the lawyer are now wide open—blood vessels beginning to rupture them. Then, there is one last gurgle from the lawyer. It is finished; the lawyer is still now. Victim number thirteen is finally complete.

Russ holds his hovering position over his prey for a few minutes. How he missed that look; cold; hypnotic; dead. Russ pats the lawyer on the cheek saying, "We will meet again one day, brother. But don't you worry … you will soon have some company. You two can pick up where you left off."

Russ stands up, admiring his handiwork from a different viewpoint. He looks around the room and notices a small fire starting on the floor by the far side of the dresser but does not bother to put it out. After he kills the whore, he will leave both bodies here to burn. He takes in three deep breaths—feeling another rush coming on—and heads to the bathroom door.

Russ begins to talk to the escort from the other side of the bathroom door.

"Hey in there, darlin', your friend is dead out here. It was a lot of fun playin' with him but the thought of playin' with you too, has forced me to end the game prematurely with him. You hear me in there? Aw, c'mon now, you really don't think that ignoring me is gonna save your ass now, do you? Huh?"

Russ begins to become a little agitated at the silence of his prey. He punches the door and detects a small gasp. "So, you are still in there and you can hear me, huh? Well, we can do this, two ways. You can: one, open the door and let the big, bad wolf in or two, you can cower in there as I huff and puff and break the fuckin' door down! One way or the other, you will soon accompany your friend out here."

There is an uncomfortable silence as Russ places an ear closer to the door to listen. The door opens slowly; the escort is standing there with both hands behind her back. Russ stands there and begins to grin. He then turns to see the sink. The hot water is running because he can now see the steam rising. He looks to her as her left hand is coming from behind her. She splashes Russ in the face with a full cup of the hot water. She begins to run from the bathroom as Russ stumbles back—hands to his face and screaming in pain. She makes it past him but stops in her tracks. She spots the lawyer on the floor, looking up to the ceiling, neither moving nor breathing.

Suddenly, she finds herself falling back. Russ has a handful of her hair, pulling her so violently, she leaves the ground. He flings her against the wall, making a loud thud. In a flash, she is up and scampering across the bed. Russ dives for her, interrupting her course and slamming her into the headboard. The two of them go into a roll and tumble off the bed.

Russ is on top of her now with both hands around her neck. Even with a red, quickly scalding face, Russ begins to grin as he always does before killing his victims.

"I have to admit it, darlin', you were a better challenge than your friend over there."

Suddenly, there was a flash of light. The fire which first started at the far side of the dresser has now spread to the curtains. This was all the distraction Gabrielle needed.

She pulls her right hand—which he had pinned to her side—loose and stabs Russ in the side with a small pocketknife. The force of the stabbing causes Russ to lean to his right, affording her the opportunity to use his weight to her advantage. Russ attempts to re-establish his position when Gabrielle pulls her legs up and around the neck of Russ; an exercise she knew well from aerobics training. With his and her own weight squarely on the backs of her shoulders, she clamps her legs tighter, with Russ frantically trying to reach her throat. Little did he realize, the harder he reaches for her, the tighter her lock on him becomes. Russ did not realize it was his own weight working against him. He begins gasping for air as her grip becomes more secure.

"How do you like being choked, you bastard? Does it feel good to you?"

Angered by this, Russ begins to work even harder to free himself so he can then, take great pleasure in wringing her neck. Gabrielle starts laughing at his feeble attempts to free himself. *You're killing yourself with your own weight, asshole. That's it … keep going … you are doing well.*

Completely secured by her grip with the last of his strength beginning to drain, she makes sure she has his attention.

"And by the way jerk, my name isn't darlin' … It's Gabrielle … and you … can … go … to … hell!"

There was a loud snap, followed by some crunching. The combination of strength in her legs and Russ' own weight causes his neck to break. Gabrielle shifts her weight, causing Russ to fall over, right beside the lawyer; now both, staring up at the ceiling.

Picking herself up, Gabrielle goes over to the nightstand and grabs her handbag. She walks over to both bodies and look down to address them.

"Well boys, it is too hard to tell who the real marks were tonight … Carson and me or you two … whoever you are. Something else I find

hard understanding is … you (looking at the lawyer) get to become a Guardian … I have no idea what position (looking at Russ) you qualify for and all I get for this is a possible promotion to Enforcer. I guess even in hell it's a 'Man's world'. I'll see you two on the battlefield, boys. It's time for me to leave … it's getting a little hot in here."

She leaves the motel room as it becomes fully engulfed in flames.

Epilogue: A word from Warden Tannenbaum

So, Russ is no longer a resident of this world. That motel room was burned to a crisp along with Russ and that lawyer guy, Harding. Gabrielle really covered her tracks by letting that room go up in flames. There will be no traces of anything or anyone because it is extremely difficult to put out hellfire. I also had to provide a stand-in for Russ here at the prison. It would be difficult—even for me to explain why Russ' body turned up in a hotel fire, now wouldn't it? Oh yeah, I almost forgot to tell you … I lied to Russ about his father. He made it to that other place but I felt it was a convincing touch.

The torture I designed for Russ is simple. Each of his victims will take turns (I made sure Russ only killed people he would one day, see again) skinning him … one strip at a time … over and over again … forever.

After that torture, Russ should make a decent Foot Soldier. Now that I have added Russ to the line up, it is time to move on to my next recruit. Are you familiar with déjà vu?

*"The wicked prowl on every side,
when vileness is exalted among
the sons of men."*

PSALM 12:8

CHAPTER 1

❧

In Middlesex County, somewhere between Monroe Township and East Brunswick, resides a school for young men. The name of this school is called Jamesburg School for Boys. This is the type of school designed for the 'troubled' and sometimes 'incorrigible' young men. A young man could be sent to Jamesburg for many reasons, particularly, for not complying with the rules of state and/or society. That is where I met Carson, "B&E," Harding.

Carson Harding was transferred to Jamesburg when he was thirteen. Since the age of ten, he had been a handful for his mother who worked at the Blakely Laundry in the late 70's and part-time at the Holiday Inn on W. State Street. Both jobs eventually closed, packed up, and moved elsewhere, leaving his mother jobless with nothing to depend on except welfare. His father—a gambler and stick-up artist—was shot and killed robbing a gas station on Calhoun Street when Carson was eight.

Carson was a shy and quiet kid who later grew ashamed of his mother for being a 'welfare case' and having to use food stamps to buy groceries. Whenever he and his mother would go to the corner store, there was always—with Carson—a sense of dread that sooner or later, one of his friends from the neighborhood would see his mother using that 'substandard' form of currency even though his mother was not alone in this neighborhood, receiving this funding. From that point, he would have to prepare himself for an eternity of 'ribbing' from most of the neighborhood. For this, Carson would hold nothing but contempt for his mother.

Carson began skipping school and hanging out with the neighborhood thugs. He would steal candy from the stores but soon graduated to pick-pocketing people while pretending to shop. He and his cronies began 'huffing' model airplane glue and paint thinners. He loved the dizzy and sometimes hallucinogenic effects he experienced; it also helped him forget about his life and poverty-stricken circumstances thereof.

By the time he was thirteen; Carson stopped attending Thomas Jefferson Elementary School and became a full-time thief. His daily routine consisted of 'huffing' some type of inhalant from a paper bag and then sneaking into someone's home to rob them. He and his friends would take the merchandise to the neighborhood 'fence'—a man called Slippery—who would pay the boys for their hard work. This went on for many months. But sooner or later—no matter how careful a thief thinks he is—a time will come when he will be careless.

It was the Fourth of July and there was a parade and music in the park commemorating 'America's Independence'. Everyone in town were in attendance; almost everyone. Carson had decided that since everyone was preoccupied with the festivities, he would seize this opportunity to supplement his presently, depleted income. This time he chose the home of Ben Evans, who worked at the motor pool of Trenton's finest.

Carson found an open window facing the alleyway between Sweets and Fountain Avenue. Once inside, he made his way up the stairs and down the hall to the back bedroom. He checked the nightstands, an armoire, and finally the closet. He began stuffing his pockets with a pair of his and her watches, three gold rings—one with a really nice diamond—a couple bangles, assorted costume jewelry, and some change on the dresser. He then returned downstairs, checking the kitchen cabinets and a sugar bowl on the counter by the toaster. He then went into the dining room, removing a tray of silverware from the base of the china cabinet. He went over to a maple, double-door server which did not match the walnut china cabinet and began rummaging through that. In the rear on the right side he pulled out an old White Owl cigar box. Inside the box he found $127.00.

Once he found this large sum of money, he quickly stuffed the bills in his pants pocket and left the way he came in. He peeked out of the window, looking into the alley in both directions. He should have just gone out of the back door. But Carson had the mindset of an opossum—an opossum can be a few inches of crossing a road but if a car approaches, the opossum will turn and head back the way it came, thinking it is the shorter, safer distance—that is why you see so many opossum carcasses on the road.

Because of the festivities, the police had been briefed to double back on the areas they patrol, thus, changing the routine and thereby, catching any 'perps' who are aware of a patrolman's normal routine.

Well, it certainly worked. Halfway out of the window a patrol car came down Sweets Avenue and slowed as it approached the alley.

The patrolman then caught a glimpse of two legs, jockeying for the small plastic milk crate which made getting into the window possible.

The patrolman stopped, put the car in reverse, and then drove slowly into the alley as Carson planted both feet on the ground. He turned and almost fell backwards at the sight of two policemen staring at him with guns drawn. This would be the first of many 'breaking and entering' arrests made on him.

By the time Carson was sixteen, he had been in and out of juvenile detention four times. As a result, he had been sentenced to serve thirty-four months, of which twenty-four would be mandatory.

CHAPTER 2

Life at Jamesburg appeared real simple. A day at Jamesburg consisted of a 6:15a.m. Wake-up; this gives an inmate fifteen minutes to get dressed, make his bed, shower (although most shower at night), and brush his teeth. At 6:35 the inmates had to be in formation for (P/T) Physical Training or a combination of P/T and (S/P) Spiritual Therapy—for inmates who claim specific religions like that of the Muslim order. Breakfast is served at 7:00, alternating the "A" shift first, then "B" shift on even days. After breakfast all inmates have roughly 25 minutes to use the restroom, clean their dormitories and report to a variety of classes including subjects like math, reading comprehension, art, carpentry, auto mechanics, and even special education courses for inmates labeled, 'cognitively deficient'. Lunch is scheduled at 12:30 p.m. with classes resuming at 1:50 p.m. Classes are completed at 3:45 p.m. unless you have tutoring sessions. Job functions begin at 4:00 p.m. and end at 6:30 p.m. Dinner is from 6:45 to 7:55 p.m. the inmates are given free time from 8:00 to 10:00 p.m. Showers are from 10:00 to 11:00, with lights out at 11:05 p.m. Weekends involve more time for job functions, free time, and visitation. Sundays include morning worship and church services for those who prefer it. All the things the normal student would be afforded with the exception of, psychological and behavioral therapies to gain some understanding why these young men need attend this modality of schooling in the first place.

Carson had some difficulty adapting to structure and remained rebellious the first six months at this institution. For this negative behavior he spent some time in Administration Segregation, or what the young men at this school referred to as, 'The Hole'. This behavior also required that he attend two, one-hour sessions for Behavioral Therapy, weekly.

It was a typical Monday afternoon when Carson found himself heading down the east wing corridor at Jamesburg. In his right hand he held an index card with a name and office number. As he walked he noticed some

of the names and titles on each door. One door read, "Suzette Ciani, MSW, Rational-Emotive Therapy." Another read, "Montgomery Borges, PhD, Family/Crisis Counseling. He finally approached the office which matched the index card reading, "Richard Sterling, PhD, Clinical Psychiatry."

Carson opened the door, walked in and saw me sitting behind a desk, head down, writing on some yellow legal. Before Carson could utter a word I asked, "Hasn't anyone ever taught you it is customary to knock on a door and wait to be invited in?"

Carson's only reply was, "Yeah, whatever man," and decided to stand his ground.

I then, took my sweet time, writing in my pad then slowly looked up, locking eyes with Carson. We continued to look at one another— unblinking; unflinching—as if we were playing a game of, "Who blinks first." The lights overhead—long cylindrical fluorescents found in most schools and businesses—went dim, causing Carson to lose his gaze and look up. The lights returned to their usual, artificially bland and ominous position. Carson, realizing he flinched first, looked around the room, taking his time returning his gaze to me behind the desk. When he did, he found me now, with a victorious grin, sitting back in my high-back, black leather chair.

"Shall we try this again?" I believe in beginning a … friendship off on a good note. What do you think about that?"

With that said, Carson turned and exited the office, closing the door behind him. He began walking in the direction from which he came, muttering words hardly audible to anyone within earshot. Midway down the corridor, he stopped and thought about the consequences for not attending these sessions. He turned and proceeded, once again, towards his previous destination. But this time he stood outside and waited.

He then, very carefully leaned putting his ear to the door to hopefully hear something which could give him the advantage. He heard nothing except an ink pen scratching on paper. *Probably writing about me,* he thought. He conceded and knocked on the door.

"Come in," my voice called out.

This time as he entered, I gradually stood and came from behind the desk. I am a man who stands about six feet, four inches tall, slender in

build, with black hair—graying on the sides but neatly groomed—with an also, graying mustache and beard—the style—a mock resemblance of Freud.

I then approach Carson and extend my right hand.

"You must be Carson Harding. I am most pleased to meet you. My name is Richard Sterling. I am one of the psychiatrists employed at this school."

Carson gave what I recognized as a half-hearted handshake, saying absolutely nothing.

"Well, I guess this is as good a start as any. "Please, have a seat so we can begin."

Carson looked around the office, hoping to find a seat as far and away as possible but the only other chair in the room was right in front of my desk. Carson began to slide the chair when I said, "I would appreciate it if you left the chair exactly where it is … that way, neither of us would have to shout to each other."

Carson continued to slide the chair to a distance, halfway between the desk and office door.

Now, standing by the side of my desk I remark, "Well, I guess that is a compromise I'm willing to defer … for now." I return to my seat behind the desk, reach for a short stack of files on the far right side, and remove the one from the top of the stack. I begin leafing through the many pages of the chart, occasionally looking up at Carson. Meanwhile, Carson sat motionless except, a few times looking at the dish of Starlite Peppermints on my desk. Noticing this, I say, "Yes, you may have a mint … help yourself."

Carson reaches over and grabs a handful, shoving them in the top left pocket of his work shirt, save one, which he begins to unwrap and shove in his mouth.

Finally, I close the chart and say, "You and I have something in common here. Your job is to tell me about the things you do and my job is to try to help you understand why. You have to complete twenty sessions with me and the first session does not begin until you make up your mind to cooperate. So, in a nutshell … sorry, poor choice of words … what I mean is you can be done here in ten weeks or ten months. And if memory

serves me correctly, you have less than six months left here. But only if you complete your treatment … so, what's it going to be, Mr. Harding?"

Not requiring much thought as to what was explained to him, Carson accedes. "Where do we begin?"

"We begin at the beginning … a fresh start."

CHAPTER 3

A few weeks pass and Carson has become comfortable talking to me, partly because I am probably the first real adult who actually ever listened to what Carson ever had to say and how he actually felt. Carson, although he knew I was paid to listen to others' problems, felt there was something else—an understanding—an identification or kinship even, to the life of one who once, traveled a similar road.

After sharing a sick and distasteful joke with me involving blood and sperm donation, I seized the opportunity to ask Carson a few questions, not necessarily in the interest of treatment but about life in general.

"The B&E's you committed … how did you know which houses were appropriate? I mean, most people either have someone home or a guard dog or even some type of electronic security while they are away."

"True … one of the things I would do is walk up to the front door and knock. If someone came to the door I would make up a name and ask if that person was home. Of course, they would tell me I have the wrong house. But if I knocked and no one answered, I would simply find an open window somewhere and climb in. One time I sneaked inside a house, bagged a few items from downstairs, tip-toed upstairs and heard a shower running and music coming from the bathroom. I thought about high-tailing it outta there but realized I could ransack the bedroom while listening to the shower and music. I knew once the shower stopped, I'd better get outta there.

I sometimes laugh when I think of that person getting out of the shower, going to bedroom and no longer seeing his money, watch or ring on the dresser. I can see him running downstairs and seeing his front door wide open. I see him going out on the porch in just a towel and looking up and down the street as if, he just might see the perpetrator."

"You know, only a special kind of person could actually pull that type of job off the way you did," I said to him with a hint of admiration.

"You're right … they call that special kind of person, 'street grease'."

"I am not referring to the deed itself but the manner in which it was done. Just think about it … even with someone in the home, you kept a cool head … didn't panic. You kept your wits about the entire situation. That, young man, is a quality held in high regard anywhere on this planet. It is a gift you would be a fool to waste."

"So, what you're sayin' is, it's okay to steal?"

"I am not implying that at all. I am merely stating that there are hundreds of legitimate professions where that gift would be best suited. There is no profession known to man where that gift would be a liability. It would be shameful to waste such a gift."

"Some gift … I think you forgot that same gift got me locked up."

"The gift didn't get you locked up, your arrogance did. You grew cocky, arrogant, and stopped paying attention to detail. You became impulsive and overconfident. You jumped out of the airplane and did not realize—until it was too late—that you failed to put on your parachute. Intelligence, backed by common sense, increases your perception. You have talents and skills you have not yet begun to realize."

"But I didn't even finish school."

"So, finish school. Only thing stopping you from doing that is you."

"What then … a job in some factory?"

"Only a coward would sell himself so short. You could do a lot more. What are you afraid of, Mr. Harding?"

"I aint' afraid of shit!" Carson snapped.

Nonsense … we are all afraid of something. The key to conquering fear is, knowing where it comes from. If you know the cause, you can develop a cure. Life, love, money, and power; all overshadowed by fear. And all the things that man is afraid to lose. The sooner you accept this, the better off you will be."

CHAPTER 4

Nineteen sessions later and Carson has shown progress. The results on his behavior prove to be prodigious. From addressing his thoughts and feelings on a somewhat dysfunctional family unit to how he views the world itself. Over the years I have been an acclaimed psychotherapist, with a highly favorable success rate for turning around youth once classified as, "Highly Resistant," to treatment. Many of my books on the psychology of children and adolescent behavior are currently being used throughout the country at many colleges and universities. With Carson and his current positive progress, I will be adding another notch on my belt.

Carson Harding walks down the east wing corridor for his final session. He recalls so many weeks ago when his thoughts were on hating to be a part of what he once called a, "Mental ass-fucking," and how he would do all he could to go down fighting. But this time his thoughts are totally different. He is beginning to look at things in a more affable respect. He has gone from borderline incorrigible to sufficiently amiable. As a matter of fact, he is actually looking at me differently than the 'toadie' Carson once envisioned me to be. Only now, at his last session, does he realize how fortunate it was for him to meet someone like me.

He knocks on the door and awaits an invitation. He is then instructed to enter. He walks in, says hello, and takes a seat beside the desk.

I decided to begin the conversation with, "Not too long ago you were extremely apprehensive and distrusting and now you look forward to our sessions. I would say that is progress. How are you feeling today, Mr. Harding?"

"I'm doing okay," he replied. "I feel a little strange though. I've been looking forward to this day and yet, I'm a little ..."

"Sad to see this day come to an end? It is okay for you to express all emotions. As I have said before, a man must ..."

"Be attuned to everything he feels," replied Carson.

"I am pleased to hear you have not begun to forget what you have learned."

"No way," replied Carson. "I intend to use all you have given me to my advantage. My only real worry now is my next phase of treatment and who my counselor will be. Will this person do what's in my best interest or will they sweep me under the rug and collect a paycheck?"

"All I can suggest to you is that you use your instincts. Your instincts allow you to make the right decisions with everything and everyone you encounter. Never second guess them ... ever."

Carson begins to chuckle in a manner I find mildly contemptuous.

"You find this all funny, Mr. Harding?"

"No, not at all ... it's just ... you sound like Obi-Wan Kenobi."

"And just who is Obi-Wan Kenobi?"

"He's a Jedi Master who mentored this kid in learning to use 'The Force'. It's a special power which takes concentration and instinct."

"Sounds like one hell of a master. Does this kid learn about this, 'Force'?"

"Sure does ... he becomes a powerful Jedi Knight and a formidable leader in the Alliance."

"What is the premise of this movie?"

"Premise?" Carson inquires.

"The story line ... what is this movie about?"

"Oh, it's a basic 'good versus evil' type of movie which takes place in a future galaxy. You gotta check it out."

"I just may do that. Seeing how we are on the subject of good versus evil, what are your thoughts about it? For instance, do you believe in heaven and hell?"

"Well, I have heard many different stories from places like Sunday school ... those few times I couldn't duck out of going. And then there are a couple of shows which talk about where we go when we die."

"And so, how do you feel about the information you have received thus far? Are you or are you not a believer?"

"I don't know and I really don't give a damn," replied Carson.

I sit back in my chair, giving Carson and his statement some perused consideration. After about twenty or thirty seconds pass I lean forward in my chair, closing the gap between me and Carson to less than two feet, purposely, breeching 'man's personal space' rule.

"Whether you believe or not will make a difference in how you see things … how you will begin to apply certain things to your world. Knowing that something awaits you at the end of your journey will help you decide how you will live your life."

"Are you sure you haven't seen 'Star Wars', Mr. Sterling? Because it sounds like you have. I mean, all you're really missing is a light saber and a cloak."

I begin to chuckle lightly at the prospect of wearing a cloak in this life. "I can assure you that I have yet to see this movie but am becoming more intrigued to do so. The fact is most educators or mentors have this air of confidence about them. It comes from those before them and personal experience. In the end, however, the choice is ultimately yours."

"I still think you saw the movie," Carson says grinning.

I walk over to the bookcase in my office—almost as tall and as wide as the wall itself—and simultaneously, pull one book from the third shelf with my left hand and another book from the fourth shelf with my right. I take a confirming glance at both books and return to my desk—both books now, resting in my lap.

"Although there are many books written on these two subjects, there are none as controversial as, 'The Holy Bible' and the 'Satanic Bible'. Both books are equally important I believe. One is allegedly good and the other allegedly, evil. Which is which, would depend on the reader."

"Well, it is obvious 'The Holy Bible' is the good one," remarks Carson.

"Are you certain of this? Have you researched either of these books? Have you ever wondered whether or not those before us got it right? Why is day, considered light and night considered dark? Why is snow cold and fire hot? You must always question and even challenge what you are told about any subject. You stated earlier the 'Holy Bible' is the good one but you also stated that you don't give a damn. I sense a degree of conflict and uncertainty in you."

Carson places one hand over the other, leans forward, and rests his chin as if to ponder what I had just revealed to him. He looks at both books, now on the desk in front of him. I hand both books to him.

"There are many paths one can take to discover the truth, Mr. Harding. I suggest you begin by researching what is already in print. From there,

the mind and heart should provide you with all that you will require. As I stated before … it is just a matter of perception."

The termination session continues and Carson and I are tying up a few loose ends; a small but relatively important matter of determining the next level of care being considered for the young Mr. Harding. Surprisingly enough, Carson would like to take a shot at the world of academia—a selection which pleases him as well as Mercer County Probation. At the end of his stay here at Jamesburg, he should have his G.E.D. as well as, the scores from his S.A.T.; all made possible by a grant courtesy of, "The Second Chance," program.

The session is officially over and I congratulate Carson on how much he had accomplished in such a short time.

"I think you should know, Mr. Harding, that many of my colleagues felt—and I really should not be telling you this—you had a, 'snowballs chance in hell', of moving through this program on a positive note. I, on the other hand, knew in my heart that you were more than capable of … how do I say this … exceeding others' expectations?"

Carson allows a hint of a smile to quickly flash across his face. He smiles not because of the compliment given him, but the mere idea of proving people wrong; a newly discovered talent he hopes to improve on in the years to come.

"I believe there is a lot more to Mr. Harding than he realizes and one day the world may come to realize it also. And I say this with heartfelt admiration."

"I only have you to thank for that," replied Carson. "I know our sessions are over now but is it okay for me to, from time to time, stop by and say hello?"

"I would be disappointed if you didn't. Besides, how will I know your thoughts, feelings and beliefs on the two books, if you did not come back down these halls? I mean, you could write but I believe direct correspondence and debate is called for on this particular matter, do you agree?"

"Absolutely … it would drive me nuts wondering and waiting. I mean, I could call but I don't do too well on the phone."

"And neither do I, Mr. Harding. I find being up close and personal minimizes the lies and deception."

I walk up to Carson; shake his right hand while placing my left hand on Carson's shoulder. As he turns and heads for the door, I say to him, "Oh, by the way, you will be a part of the graduating ceremonies in May, right?"

"Not only will I be graduating, I intend to receive the Valedictorian. I hope you can attend."

"I wouldn't miss your graduation for the world, Mr. Harding. I like to think I had a hand in your achievement. But only a small hand. The rest is all you."

Carson nods and heads through the door and down the hall. I return to my desk and pull the bottom right drawer open. I remove two books from the drawer and head over to the bookcase. Once again, I place one book on the third shelf with my left hand, and the other book on the fourth shelf with my right hand, respectively.

I return to my desk and sit down. *Phase two complete and Phase three in motion.*

CHAPTER 5

Several years have passed since Carson Harding's incarceration at Jamesburg. He has, to date, become one of the success stories from that school. Most young men come through that institution only to graduate to more serious crime and as a consequence, graduate to adult incarceration; that is, those who are not killed, 'living by the sword'. A large percentage of those young men will wind up in places like Bayside, Rahway, and Trenton State Prison—the absolute big time—but Carson's fate, that is not.

Carson kept his promise. He kept a continual contact with me. I helped him with an enrollment to Mercer County Community College, a transfer to Rider College, (now a university) and finally, an admission to Georgetown where Mr. Harding is enrolled as a law student, nearing completion.

Meanwhile, I do my best in keeping up with my altruistic appearances, influencing faculty at Georgetown and setting a predetermined reservation at a prestigious law firm in New York, with offices located throughout the eastern United States. I often relish at the thought that soon my investment will begin to pay out extremely large dividends. After all, I should feel this way. My investments in people have always paid handsomely.

Time again, has passed and Carson continues to keep his promise as I have kept mine. Carson is now a member at the law offices of Aronberg, Pressler, and Cohen. The law firm is not one bit surprised with how Mr. Harding tackles his caseload with efficiency, graceful precision, and an infallible knowledge of the law; past and present.

Nine months pass at the firm when he is given a 'Pro Bono' case classified as, "Unwinnable." This was the case of, "The United States vs. Jeremy Smith," a reputed drug dealer who allegedly killed an undercover police officer who had infiltrated his organization. According to the prosecution, Mr. Smith was voice recorded, filmed, his fingerprints on the murder weapon, and last—and equally important—a black man.

The firm believed it was time for Mr. Harding to put a check mark in the 'loss column' and decided to offer as little help to him as possible. The firm needed to see how Mr. Harding would perform under this type of pressure. Not to mention, it would be a, "Slap in the face," to 'yours truly' who, constantly runs interference with the firm. For some members of the firm, it would prove to be an admonished irony.

Would Carson be capable of enduring the monotony and misery of being assigned lost causes? Even a modicum of composure would be all the firm would need to know that, my protégé is all they were told he would be.

Nevertheless, Harding created one hell of a defense. First, by looking into the background of two of the four cops, he discovered prior I.A. reports suggesting these two cops were not as clean-cut or racially impartial as the jury and prosecution would have wanted. Harding used the 'race card' to discredit the cops which, in the near future, opened the floodgates to many convicts, apprehended by said cops. Secondly, Harding had to discredit the fingerprint analysis so he hired an expert in the field to convince the jury that these partial prints could easily belong to at least ten other people.

Fingerprints are identified on a point system including, an arc recognition—the more points, the greater the chance the print is yours and no one else's. Because the print on the weapon contained only five points and half an arc, it was no difficult feat to find a patsy; someone who could step in and claim the prints as theirs. It just so happens, that someone in, "The Griffin's," organization could be that patsy; a soldier who shared the same points and half-arc on his left thumb. Not to mention, if he chose not to be the scapegoat, his mother and four siblings would be dropped—accidently, of course—in a meat grinder over at the Frenchy's Horsemeat factory on Brunswick Ave.

When it was all over, Harding was the victor. He had done the impossible. This victory caused a ripple effect throughout the judicial system as well as, the underground systems. The District Attorney's office will be working overtime for the next eighteen months, handling old cases, once closed, and now re-opened for retrial. So many cases would now be overturned because of Harding—protector of the underdog.

CHAPTER 6

A year passes and Mr. Harding is now a Jr. Partner in the firm. Still undefeated, Carson has helped raise the stock at Aronberg, Pressler, and Cohen in one gargantuan leap. Most of Harding's clientele—lords of the underground—pay in cash, gold bars, and even the infamous 'Blood Stone' diamonds from the mines of Africa.

It is a warm, late afternoon when Carson's secretary buzzes him. "Mr. Harding, there is a Mr. Sterling on the phone for you."

"Thanks Jill, send it through."

"Dr. Sterling, how are things at Jamesburg?"

"Things are well, Mr. Harding … very well. I guess I do not have to ask you how things are going. I saw your picture on the front cover of 'Law Review' … Jr. Partner … a pretty big feat for someone who was once a criminal. All the folks here are extremely proud of you, Mr. Harding."

"Thanks," Carson replied. "I owe it all to my best friend and teacher … you may know the man … he resembles you in so many ways."

I laugh and immediately interject. "Hey, I told you before, I merely pointed you in the direction of the door … it was you who made the decision to take the necessary steps to walk through that door."

"Say what you want but I know I could not have done any of it without you. So, to what great pleasure do I owe this call?"

"Well, I am in town today and tomorrow and was wondering if you would join me for dinner?"

Without hesitation Carson replied, "Name the place and time and I will be there."

"How does seven at Copernicus' sound to you?"

"Sounds like you have a dinner date. You mind giving me a small hint as to what this is all about?"

"I thought it would be nice to just catch up on things with my favorite protégé … nothing more, nothing less."

"You forget I'm a lawyer who lies for a living so, I can smell an untruth or a half-truth a mile away."

"Okay, you got me, but not on the phone. I prefer being up close and personal, remember?"

"I do," replies Carson. "I will see you at seven ... sharp."

Carson returns the phone to its cradle and rings his secretary.

"Yes, Mr. Harding, how may I help you?"

"Do me a favor Jill and clear my calendar for the rest of the day. Also, no more calls from anyone okay?"

"As you wish, Mr. Harding ... will you require anything else?"

"Yes, you can go home early for a change. I will be in late tomorrow, so I will see you at 10:30."

"Thank you, sir and have a good evening."

CHAPTER 7

Harding arrives at Copernicus' at 6:57. The Maitre "D" greets him and tells him his party is already here and seated. Harding is escorted through the dining area, receiving looks, head nods, and raised glasses from people who know him or know of him. Harding then spots me seated in the best spot the house has to offer. Harding is escorted there, his hat and overcoat taken, he slides into a nicely padded nook, adjacent to me.

"Nice table," Harding says while giving the area a once over. "Don't know if I could get this table on my own. As a matter of fact, I doubt that any of the Senior Partners could get this table. It seems to me, there are no limits to your ... prestige."

I flash my familiar smile. "The owner and I go back a really long way. We have known one another since the emergence of the Bronze Age."

"Well, I hope you are referring to the Western Civilization History course you two both took back in college. After all, that was a B.C. period which would make you two, older than dirt."

"As I said before, we have known each other a really long time, Mr. Harding."

"Ahem," Harding clears his throat and changes the subject. "So, what type of meeting is this ... personal, business, or both?"

"I think a little bit of both is necessary. After all, it has been some time since you and I put our heads together to conquer anything."

"And just what, pray tell, is it that we need to now conquer?"

"Oh, the usual stuff ... complacency, division, oppositional defiance, and mutiny."

"Sounds a little esoteric, if you asked me ... how about you trim the fat a little and tell me what is really on your mind."

"My real concern is for you, Mr. Harding. To date, you have done well for yourself but I sense something about you ... something almost of a recidivist nature. I hope I am wrong about this."

"I assume you are referring to the investment offer from Mr. Jeremy Smith. He promises the highest yield for my money."

"He's drug dealing scum!" I bark. I glance around quickly, and regain my composure. "Mr. Harding, soon you will be propelled into a position which offers much more than money … power and prestige … by far, the greatest currency on earth. Do not jeopardize that by blinding yourself from your true ambition. Besides, you getting that piece of shit off the hook will be in vain. According to my sources, his days are truly numbered."

Harding realizes how fatuitous it was to even consider such nonsense. He had forgotten the earlier lessons taught to him back at Jamesburg. He had repressed some of those old feelings which catered to the criminal element so long ago. The firm is aware of many of the clients and how they earn a living but money is money.

I sense Harding's confusion and negative faith and realize I must reassure my protégé of how important he is. I reach across the table and place both hands on Carson's, giving them a motivational pat. Harding looks up to me and force a smile.

"Do not waste too much time beating yourself up about this, Mr. Harding. We are all guilty of this and we do fall short from time to time. What matters more is our ability not to obey such impulses."

I release my hold and sit back as the waiter brings our drinks and appetizers. Carson picks up his drink—a scotch on the rocks—and takes a sip. He takes one more sip and returns the glass to its coaster. He looks around the room and without looking at me says, "I will decline the offer this evening."

"Good, but personally, I think in the end you would have come to that conclusion on your own. Your greatness lies above ground … leave the underground to the scum and their low-life-going-nowhere lawyers."

CHAPTER 8

A car pulls up to an abandoned building, once a body shop by the canal on Old Rose Street. Two figures are in the vehicle—a 1979 Buick Electra Limited, gray with money green interior. Although the car is eight years old, it still looks brand new.

The two men inside are sharing a quart of Colt 45 malt liquor, smoking cigarettes, and listening to the radio. The guy on the passenger side has a shopping bag between his legs, lying on the floor.

A car drives by, slows its pace, and continues up the hill. The two young men watch the vehicle continue up the street, look at each other, and resume the task of smoking, drinking, and waiting.

About fifteen minutes go by when a black, Grand National rumbles up to them and parks in front of the Buick. The driver of the Grand National shuts off his engine, lights, and exits the car. He casually looks around, assessing his surroundings and lights a cigarette. Replacing the lighter in his left top pocket of his Tommy Hilfiger shirt, he slowly walks to the Buick. After standing at the car and talking to the driver, the man on the passenger side gets out and walks to the rear of the car, looks around, and proceeds to walk in the direction of the canal which is about twenty yards away. The driver moves the shopping bag from the floor to his lap while the driver of the Grand National enters from the passenger side.

The guy at the canal looks at his watch, studying it in the fashion of some synchronized countdown. He quickly guzzles the rest of the beer and smashes the bottle against the cement retaining wall of the canal's catwalk—simultaneously in perfect unison—to the sound of a shotgun blast. He begins to walk at a quickened pace in the direction of both cars. The passenger exits the car with the shopping bag and quietly closes the door. The other man—already at the Grand National—opens the driver's door, gets in, and starts the car. He is joined by the previous driver of the Grand National who now sits on the passenger side. The Grand National pulls off, leaving the Buick Electra, as well as its now dead driver, in the darkness.

CHAPTER 9

Still at the restaurant Carson Harding and I are in the middle of the main course when I decide to switch the conversation from business to personal.

"Mr. Harding, I was wondering if you ever found time to finish those two books I gave you so long ago?"

"As a matter of fact, I have read each one several times. I found both books extremely well-written pieces of fiction."

"Do I detect a modicum of ambivalence, Mr. Harding?"

"I guess you could call it that. After all, we are talking about religion here. In my experience, I have come to realize how vague and figurative all religious doctrine tend to be. Truth is … no one really knows how most of these stories are created, so, we can only go by this person's interpretation or that person's theories."

"Well, if you had to choose one to follow … which one would be more favorable?"

"This sounds strangely close to a 'loaded question'."

"Not at all, Mr. Harding … I believe one book could not survive without the other. That, my friend, is a small part of how I interpreted both texts. My question was and still is … which would you choose?"

"I am not really sure about either, to tell you the truth. Both texts demand that I serve some type of deity. I like to think of myself as my own master—in great accompaniment of other masters—making my own luck and designing my own fate … controlling my own destiny, if you will. Not some lost, mindless being doing everything by order of some power that will reward me in the afterlife. Talk about being deceived—the Ten Commandments and the Eleven Satanic Rules … that's what I call, 'getting bent over and royally reamed'."

"It sounds to me, like you have truly done quite a bit of research on this subject, Mr. Harding."

"Well, I've done enough to convince myself that religion is a total waste of time, energy, and most of all, money. People—all over the world—are killing each other in the name of their God."

"It sounds like the Satanic Bible would suit you far better than the Holy Bible."

"Actually, I prefer the scientific explanation … that we are 'aimlessly racing towards nothingness'."

"So, what you are saying is that when this life is over, there is nothing … no heaven … no hell … not even a limbo. We can go ahead and spend those two coins instead of placing them on the eyes of the dead for the Ferry Man?"

"If there was such a thing as a Ferry Man, he would be wanted by the IRS for an eternity of tax evasion."

I begin to laugh, shaking my head with somewhat amiable consideration. "I must admit, Mr. Harding, the bible does ask man to give up a lot of things to earn a ticket to this place called heaven. And almost everything man does seem to carry with it, some degree of peccavi. And being a lawyer—a successful one—forces you to break almost every commandment in the book."

"What puzzles me most is how in the New Testament, God was everywhere and he spoke to everyone—Adam, Abraham, Isaac, Jacob, Moses, Noah—you name it, He was there. Then, He just disappeared or forgot we were still here. Today, if someone claims to have heard God speak, we would lock them up in some psychiatric hospital and give them a shot of Haldol or Thorazine for their trouble. And what about all those miracles we either read or heard about … the parting of the Red Sea, Noah's Ark, and Jonah in the belly of a whale? Have we fallen from grace so much that we are no longer privy or worthy of sights and miracles such as these?"

"Mr. Harding, if you witnessed a miracle like the ones you have mentioned, would you be convinced of His existence?"

"I would probably become a believer. But it has to be a true miracle … something that cannot be explained as something else … a bonafide, honest-to-goodness, miracle."

"Maybe this God wants you to have faith and just believe."

"And what if I chose to believe ... what then? What good can come from it to ask forgiveness for sins I am destined to continue committing until I retire or die? The book says to ask forgiveness from God and your soul will be saved. You mean to tell me that if Hitler asked for forgiveness, he would be able to enter heaven with Martin Luther King Jr.? That he would be side by side with Moses and Jesus? I don't know about you, but there has to be a fine print ... some type of disclaimer at the bottom of that proclamation."

"I believe you are probably right, Mr. Harding. I should have known better than to debate anything with a lawyer."

The waiter approaches and asks if there is anything else he can get for us. We both nod to the contrary. The waiter places the leather billfold on the end of the table, motions for the busboy and quietly exits.

"I am so pleased that my evening was not a boring, total loss. How I miss our little discussions, Mr. Harding."

"Likewise, Mr. Sterling, but it seems to me, we always leave things ... half resolved."

"So, what is your answer ... if you had to choose a text to follow ... which one would it be?"

"Not the Holy Bible," replied Carson.

"I think we are continuing to make progress, Mr. Harding."

CHAPTER 10

It's a cool, but lovely Friday morning and Mr. Harding decides to work from home. He occasionally does this when he has a major case approaching with the court date set, for that following Monday. Most professionals, in high power positions adhere to a superstition. Carson spends the entire Friday before a Monday court date in his blue silk pajamas by Bali, Beverly Hills. He has his usual for breakfast—a cheese and mushroom omelet, wheat toast with grape jelly, milk, and tops that off with a Bloody Mary; extra Tabasco. During this breakfast, he checks his messages, double-checks his mail from the previous day, and watches the channel 10 news. Most of the time, it's just the usual chaos and his favorite sports teams blowing a game in the final seconds. But this morning's news caught his attention a little more than usual.

"We begin this news broadcast from the Lincoln Homes section of Trenton. An undercover officer was discovered slain last night in an unknown vehicle. The officer was allegedly executed and robbed by a known felon. Anthony Thomas, of the North 25 section of Trenton was apprehended late last night along with a shotgun which, may have been the weapon used on the officer. Anthony Thomas is one of the many convicted criminals whose case was overturned as a result of the 'United States vs. Jeremy Smith' trial, where a few crooked cops had been exposed. The identity of the officer will not be released until his family is notified. There may have been another assailant involved but police have yet to confirm the information given them. Our prayers go out to the family of this officer while we try to understand why the legal system works in favor of the offender instead of the victims. This is Mike Brentmore, coming to you live from the Lincoln Homes section in Trenton ... back to you, Connie."

After hearing the name of the alleged shooter, and the rest of that particular news story, Harding picks up the remote and hits the mute button, sitting back in his leather recliner. *This makes the third time an overturned case proved tragic* he thought to him. *I guess I'll get an earful*

on Monday morning from the office of the D.A. The prosecution may even try to use this to help their case. I must find a way to use this more to my advantage … and I will.

Several days pass and Harding is as skillful and eloquent as usual during the press conference. The prosecution tried to use the, "Cop killer," card as Harding had suspected; a bad move. Mr. Harding, once again, made the undercover cop, as well as the entire operation a 'half-ass' plan of incompetence. The undercover cop's back was not covered by his operatives. No one knew he was making a deal, where the deal was being made or the names of all parties involved. Statements made would once again, place the cops under scrutiny by Internal Affairs.

On the same day and at the same time, the undercover cop, now identified as, Mark Mathis was being buried with full honors. He left to mourn him a wife, two sons, a mother, and a host of relatives and friends. Several members from Mark's unit served as pallbearers and one unit member—his best friend—gave words of encouragement, which followed the eulogy.

With Officer Mathis placed in the ground and the funeral services over, several officers got together at the local pub to drown their sorrows. While going back and forth with what happened the reception was interrupted by the news on the television. The newscaster mentioned the 'muffed' undercover operation and how it proved advantages to Mr. Harding during the press conference. Mr. Harding had once again, won at the law enforcement's expense.

This proved to be more than the unit could bear. Five of the officers move to a secluded room at the rear of the pub so they could create a new strategy—the assassination, immolation, and elimination of the invincible Carson Harding.

CHAPTER 11

Three weeks pass and Carson Harding has left the office late on a Thursday evening to enjoy a three-day weekend. All of his cases are caught up and he has nothing really pressing. He stops by the local Chinese restaurant for some takeout—Shrimp Lo Mein, Chicken Chop Suey, Kung Pao Shrimp, and six egg rolls—enough to last him the entire weekend. He pays for his food and leaves.

As he approaches his car, another car pulls up beside him. He turns and as the window slowly rolls down he notices the driver.

"Good evening, counselor," the officer says in a sarcastically, distasteful manner.

"What can I do for you, Quinn? And I hope you make it quick ... Chinese food is best eaten while hot."

"Oh, I'll make this real quick. It is guys like you who make our job so hard. You know a person is guilty, yet, you turn our personal demons into professional liability ... and for what? So you can earn enough money to move away from the same scum you prevent us from locking up."

Already bored with the conversation, Harding puts his hand to his mouth, imitating a yawning gesture. "I thought you said you were gonna be quick about this?"

Officer Quinn, now irritated says, "I only have one more thing to say ... this is for Mark and anyone else who have died or will die for what you have done."

Officer Quinn points a Government Issue .45 caliber pistol at Harding and lets off three shots, all hitting Harding in the upper torso.

Harding is knocked backwards against the driver's window as his bag of Chinese food explodes and goes off in multiple directions. Officer Quinn speeds off as patrons from inside the restaurant come into the parking lot to investigate. With his back against the front tire, Harding tries to get up but realizes he can hardly breathe. Harding completely falls over, face down, to a growing crowd.

Harding is rushed to a nearby trauma center and rushed immediately into O.R. #1. With the recorder on, the lead surgeon assesses the wounds—two GSW's to the upper right quadrant entering the right lung with no sign of an exit wound and one gun shot wound through the sternum, possibly in or close proximity to the aorta. The surgery went on for a little over four hours.

Carson is placed in the ICU and listed in critical condition. Although the surgery went as well as it could have gone, Mr. Harding is nowhere close to being out of the woods, considering the damage to his heart and lungs. Carson had been placed on a ventilator, sedated, and will be monitored throughout the night. Surgeries of this magnitude are subject to post-op complications.

Harding had been in and out of consciousness for the past twenty-four hours, while the rest of the country and legal world had been getting mixed reports of his attack and condition. Truth is, due to the extent of his injuries, the doctors who have been working on him felt he may not make it another day. The countdown to Mr. Harding's demise had begun.

"Mr. Harding, can you hear me?" I whispered to him. "Wake up, son."

Carson opens his eyes, blinking often to adjust them to the bright, fluorescent lights. He turns his head to the right and spots an assortment of flowers on the ledge of the window, the table in the corner, and a planter on the floor by a reclining chair. He looks to the left and spots a familiar face—a face he always respected and trusted. As painful as it was for Harding, he manages to force a smile.

"I won't waste your time with how you're feeling … no one feels great or even okay with three bullets in them. There's something you need to know Mr. Harding, and tomorrow will be too late to tell you."

I pull the stool closer to him—a black, padded, four legged kind on wheels—and sit on it, leaning forward and placing my right hand on Carson's left hand. Harding notices—for the first time—a look of serious concern on the face of his mentor.

"I hate to be the one to break this news to you, son but the doctors here will begin to believe that they have done all they are humanly capable of. Soon … very soon your heart will fail. One of your valves will rupture and you will bleed in your chest and the rest will spill out into this clear, plastic apparatus at the foot of your bed. That will send an immediate alert to the

nurses station and they will come in here and try, unsuccessfully I might add, to control the bleeding while the doctor attempts to resuscitate you."

Carson looks to me with wide, curious eyes. He begins to wonder why I am telling him all this. The monitor blips an irregular rhythm, startling Harding.

"I'm telling you this because I can save you. But you have to trust and believe what I'm about to tell you. Time is short, so I will be brief. If you pledge yourself to me—heart and soul—I will save your life on this day. But, the life I save will belong to me. You will do my will and no one else's. All you have to say to me is, "My soul, I freely give to you," and I will return you to the land of the living where you will become one of the most admired and revered lawyers on this planet. What say you, Mr. Harding?"

Carson uses his eyes to motion to the tube in his mouth. I nod and pull out a scroll. I point to the spot where Harding should make his mark. He tries to lift his right arm far enough to pull the scroll towards him but only manages to rest his arm on his stomach. He looks to me as if to say, "What now?"

I then take Harding's hand by the wrist and place it, palm down on the scroll. In a second, a bluish-grey smoke begins to rise from the scroll—a very thick, and pungent smoke—which makes a beeline towards the window. Even though the windows were closed, the smoke seems to fuse through the glass. I lift Carson's hand high enough to pull the document from beneath it. I roll the document up and tuck it away on the inside of my blazer.

"I know this may be somewhat confusing to you, Mr. Harding but I assure you, when the time is right, I will provide you with all the answers to your questions. I will find you when the time is right. Until that time comes Mr. Harding ... you take care."

I get up and begin to leave. I look back once more at Harding and say, "I'll have some fresh flowers delivered to you ... I'm afraid the others did not take too well to the brimstone."

Harding turns his head to the window and notices all the flowers were wilted and completely dead—even the planter on the floor beside the recliner. He returns his gaze back, only to find the room once again, empty. Harding begins to feel a pain in his chest. He hears the monitor starting to beep like crazy. The last thing he hears is the P.A. announcer saying, "Code Blue, room eleven, Code Blue, room eleven."

CHAPTER 12

As I promised, Carson makes a full recovery with the help of a lot of physical therapy including, a specialist who works with numerous patients who may suffer PTSD, as a result, of being attacked. The one thing Harding refuses to talk about in his sessions, as well as outside the sessions, the identity of the person who shot him. For some reason unknown to him, he felt it prudent to keep that information under lock and key for now.

Another of my promises was the heights he would attain in his profession. Instead of staying at the firm as a full partner, he decides to branch out and start his own firm in the New York area. A fresh start he believes he needs now. Besides, being a loner—with no familial or romantic attachments—his departure would barely go noticed. One thought which seems to plague him daily is the marker I have yet to call. It seems as if I have left the planet. I have not worked at Jamesburg for many years and made it impossible for anyone to locate me. One thing Mr. Harding knows for sure … I will hold him to that final promise; it is just a question of when …

Epilogue: A word from Dr. Richard Sterling.

The title of this story clearly tells you which position I will one day, award Mr. Carson Harding. He will be able to move in and out of this world—a connection between hell and earth—to take on human form when necessary. For now, he will remain as is—a normal, fragile human with a vast knowledge of the law. He will set the bar so high, all lawyers will be destined to one day, serve me also.

Mr. Harding's number eventually came up on a Tuesday morning, September 11, 2001 at the World Trade Center. His office was located in the North Tower—the first tower hit. Mr. Harding, like many others working on the floors directly hit by that plane, was completely incinerated. The one thing about jet fuel—it burns almost as hot as hellfire. Many of

those poor souls will go to heaven. But not my dear Mr. Harding ... he belongs to me.

I know what you're thinking. Wasn't Harding killed by Russ Jericho in a hotel room? The answer is yes. But Mr. Harding's torture consists of dying a thousand and one deaths. Fitting for lawyer, don't you think?

"Do not enter into judgment with Your servant,
For in Your sight no one living is righteous."

PSALM 143:2

CHAPTER 1

The last story should have told you how much I love lawyers. Well, if there is one thing I love more than lawyers it's those involved in politics. Remember, I have been here since the dawn of times. Ancient Rome consisted of the Caesar's; all manipulated by the Senate. It was I who seduced and influenced Caiaphas, Herod Antipas, and finally, Pontius Pilate. I forgot to mention Judas Iscariot, the apostle who became jealous of Jesus and Mary Magdalene. Oh, the thoughts—before and after the capture of Jesus—I put in that poor misguided soul.

Now, it is true that my plans to control, manipulate, and claim the Christ's soul fell through several times but nothing beats failure like a continuous try.

Back to the politics; I still believe that it is through politics that I will control the world and one day, overthrow the greatest government of all. Nostradamus was very accurate in making that prediction.

The day of Armageddon draws near. And I am still on the lookout for that political figure—one who will draw the entire earth to believe in one cause and one cause only … mine. I came pretty close with Hitler. And I am aware of how I went wrong. I underestimated many countries especially, the United States—along with those disgustingly, delusional Christians—who interfered with my plans. I became overly anxious and pushed Hitler too fast. I overlooked how mentally fragile humans are. With these new recruits I will have to take things slower; starting with this one …

CHAPTER 2

It's a Friday evening—the last day of a taxing work week. The Mayor Martin Holmesbrook is pouring himself a drink and heading to his study when the phone rings. His daughter answers the phone and yells to her father that the call is for him. He goes into the study and picks the phone up.

"I have it, sweetheart," he informs his daughter. She hangs the phone up on her end. Martin checks the buttons on his phone to make sure the line is secure.

"This is Martin, how can I help you?"

"I think you need to turn to channel eight … you may want to see this," the voice replies.

Martin grabs the remote and turns the television on. He quickly turns the channel to eight, adjusts the volume and places the remote on the table. He picks his drink up and takes a sip while the news cast continues.

"Stock markets continue to plummet as the country tries to rebound from one of the worst droughts this country has faced in many years. Experts are estimating billions of dollars in damage by the end of the year marking yet, another blow to 'Reaganomics'. On the local news, local police, teamed with ATF and DEA on a city-wide 'sting operation', seize several thousand pounds of cocaine and heroin and over a half a million dollars in cash from two separate locations on the north side. Several officers were injured during a fire fight but none were critical. Officers injured and apprehended a reputed drug dealer in the melee. Jeremy, "The Griffin," Smith was shot and wounded at one of the warehouses raided.

The Griffin is being treated for his wounds at St. Francis Medical Center and is under armed guard's protection. This raid is what many have labeled, 'First Lady Nancy Reagan's, last big push', referring to her mission to rid the country of drugs in her, 'Just Say No!' campaign which started at the beginning of her husband's first term. When we return we will have Robert Gillman with sports and a 'first' for baseball …

Martin placed the television on mute and returned to the phone. "Did you know this was going to happen tonight?" Martin inquired.

"I didn't hear about it until twenty minutes ago. Am I wrong to assume you were not informed of this raid, Mr. Mayor?"

"I did not know it was going to happen this soon," Martin replied, hesitantly.

"So I guess my next question is … how could such a maneuver be executed in your town without your knowledge or input? Can this be an act of … plausible deniability?"

Martin was dumbstruck at the questions, not wanting to say too much or too little.

"All I can say for now, is someone was a little too impulsive with this move. Our intention was the catching of one big fish to help us nab the bigger fish …"

The voice on the other end interrupted, "Well, you may have to chalk this one up as, 'the one that got away'."

"I believe we can still get the bigger fish. When Mr. Smith gets a taste of how much time he will be facing he will, without a doubt, roll over on the rest."

"Are you sure about this? The Griffin has always possessed that loyalty, we in politics, only dream of having."

"Oh, he'll roll over, play fetch, and beg when the prosecutors hang the death penalty over his head."

"I pray that you are right … because if you are not, you had better start planning on your future as the ex-Mayor. You do remember what we talked about a few months ago … don't you?"

"No, I have not forgotten that conversation … as a matter of fact, I have decided to only use that as my 'Ace in the hole'."

"I think you had better think about playing that card, real soon."

"Not yet. Politics is messy enough, without such … mudslinging. I prefer to win on the topics."

"Topics … you want to win on the topics? Do you think these insipid voters really give a damn about some topics? The environment … medical issues … the economy? You are a fool if you waste time with that viewpoint. The voters want juice … not a handful of grapes."

"Trust me on this one, Mr. Brendan ... my pen is mightier than my sword."

"We will see, Martin. I think you know what our next move should be ... can it be done?"

"You may consider it already in the works. I need to make a special call ... someone in the Governor's office owes me a favor. I will talk to you later."

"Good luck, Mr. Mayor."

Martin hangs the phone up and slams the rest of his drink down. He takes the mute off the television and turns the channel. Every other news show is discussing the raid. He turns the television off and picks up the phone again. *It is time for my special favor.*

CHAPTER 3

That following Monday brought about an uproar in jubilation for the Councilman Brennan and the local agencies involved in the sting operation. Several cops were awarded citations while others were being interviewed by Internal Affairs. There was media frenzy when the news of crooked police—along with two dirty judges—were exposed and implicated in attempting to avert or at least, delay the raid. Media and news vans were parked in front of the Police Station, Court House, and City Hall. Fortunately for the Mayor, he was not present due to a 'special commission' he was presently presiding over.

The North Ward Councilman David Brennan was at the court house answering questions and making a statement to the news and media. He promised them that his administration would do everything in its legal power to uncover all parties involved; those who received payments to look the other way or alter any legal aspects encouraging murder and drug trafficking.

Councilman David Brennan takes a ride out to Cream Ridge, New Jersey, about six or seven miles southeast of Allentown. David usually makes this trip to get away from work and any peering eyes looking for leverage on him.

He pulls up to a huge, elegant-looking rancher that was set on about twelve acres overlooking the Cream Ridge Golf Course. Although this placed appeared 'out in the open', David went through great pains to cover his tracks; switching cars and sending his vehicle elsewhere by a look-alike.

David pulled in a garage designated for him, not exiting the vehicle until the garage door fully closed. Exiting the car he went to a door which had an alpha-numeric keypad beside it. He typed in his code: E-1-A-S-P-H-O-D-E-L—something he always admired and remembered from History 205, while attending Trenton State College. The code, once accepted, allowed him passage inside and down a long corridor which

actually seemed longer than the house itself. It always amused him that the inside of this place always seemed twice as large as the rancher itself.

He met a man at the end of the corridor who recognized him, gave a short nod and opened the double doors to a room with a bar, dance floor, and in-ground Jacuzzi. Another man approached him and took his jacket. The man asked David if he would like a drink. David ordered a scotch, light on the ice. He turned and saw a friendly face.

"Good afternoon, Councilman … I trust all is going as planned?"

David walked over to me and shook my hand. The waiter brought over his drink and quietly exited the room. The two of us took a seat at a small, cozy table to the left of the bar.

"All is going as it was designed. The Griffin has fallen, Judge Chambers is under indictment and the Mayor is scrambling like a cockroach does when the light gets turned on."

Do you know if he made the call to the Governor's Aide yet?"

"If he has, he has not told me about it," I replied. "One thing I know for sure … the Griffin will give them absolutely nothing. He's far too proud to be a snitch. He wouldn't dare go out like some chump, crawling on his belly for some clemency."

"I can hardly wait to see the look on his face when he realizes his most trusted friend is actually mine. So, Mr. Brogan … what should our next step be?"

"Let us just wait and see if the Governor's Aide takes the bait and produces the planted evidence. Once that ball gets put into play, we can take them all down … 'Michael Corleone' style. In the meantime, take a rest and enjoy yourself. Your friend is here and awaits you in your special room."

David finishes his drink and leaves the bar. He heads down another hall until he reaches the first room on the right. He smoothes his hair back and enters the room. Inside the room many candles are burning, casting shadows on the black painted walls of the room. A young boy, no older than seventeen is lying on the bed, on his side, licking a Popsicle dressed in nothing but a pink Kimono.

"Eating in bed again, huh? You are such a naughty boy! I guess I'm gonna have to discipline you, again."

The boy smiles coyly and takes longer, slower licks on the Popsicle. He then takes the Popsicle and begins sliding it down his chest to his bellybutton. David closes the door, takes his belt off and walks over to the bed.

CHAPTER 4

Mayor Martin Holmesbrook makes the call to the Governor's Aide, asking for that 'special favor' which the aide was more than happy to oblige. The aide informed the Mayor that the package would be delivered to him by special courier and that he and he alone, is authorized to sign for it.

The large manila envelope is delivered, the Mayor signs for it, and it is safely put away. The Mayor would not take the chance of opening the package and exposing its contents to eyes which could possibly alert the Councilman. The Mayor had already decided to open it in the safe and secure confines of his home office.

CHAPTER 5

With the trial of 'The United States vs. Jeremy Smith' on the horizon, the resignation of Judge Chambers, and several indictments of police officers in motion, the city can now move on to the next item on its agenda—The Governor's Ball—held yearly to honor and acknowledge achievements and contributions, to the improvement and advancement of the State of New Jersey. This affair attracts all professions from journalists and businessmen to activists and civil servants; but especially, to local politicians and media.

Everyone knew that this black tie affair would be especially interesting this year; even scandalous, perhaps. The banquet committee even changed the color of the carpet from black to red, resembling Hollywood's version of the Oscars. They suspect that everybody who is somebody will attend and gladly give their thoughts on the recent events.

There seemed to be twice as many photographers and media at the affair this evening, than it had been in the past five or six years.

When Councilman David Brennan appeared on the red carpet with his wife, Elizabeth, every camera in the banquet hall began flashing. David had informed his wife earlier that this would probably happen and to be mindful not to squint or turn away from the flash; to smile and wave and nod as if she had been born to it.

The Mayor was also in attendance but came solo; his wife at home, supposedly sick. It would not take long for rumors to begin flying in regards to why the Mayor's wife was unable to attend.

The Councilman escorted his wife to their table, kissed her on the cheek, and promised her he would not leave her alone for too long. He walked over to the fountain at the end of the red carpet where photographers and media instantly began throwing a barrage of questions his way. The Governor and a CNN spokesperson joined David, taking pictures and answering questions.

The Police Commissioner from Trenton joins the Mayor at his table.

"You would think the man single-handedly brought down the Griffin, Judge Chambers, and all those once, decorated officers, by his lonesome. At this rate he'll be nominated for the Nobel Peace Prize," the commissioner said in a low voice.

The Mayor managed to smile through the commissioner's ranting.

"Everyone deserves their fifteen minutes in the spotlight. He loves to uncover others' indiscretions. I just hope he can take it as graciously as he dishes it out."

"I hate to bring this up now, Martin, but many say he has begun campaigning for your job. Are you aware of that?"

"I am well aware of that … have been for some time. And yet, I am not one bit worried about it. He's going to offer the people grapes … I will give them juice."

"And just what does that mean, Martin?"

"You will soon see … everyone will soon see … and understand."

CHAPTER 6

The Mayor was at home watching television when the anchorman announced Councilman Brennan's push for the next Mayoral election. The anchorman goes on to say to his viewers how Mayor Holmesbrook had better rescue some kittens from a tree or rush into some burning building, pulling out some elderly person—wheelchair and all—if he expects to stand a chance against Councilman Brennan. The Mayor smirks and takes a sip of his drink. The phone rings and Martin picks it up. "Hello?"

"Did you just catch that little plug on the news?" I ask Martin, rather flatly.

"I did and I thought it was a little tasteless, but necessary. It is a bittersweet delight to see so many people lifting him to such heights. The fall is going to break his neck in the end."

"Does that mean your favor was honored and the gift delivered?"

"That is a yes on both counts. Would you like to know what I know?"

"Absolutely ... today would be a nice day to know what you know. You just name the place and time and I will be there, Martin."

"The usual place at about 6:30 ... that soon enough for you?"

"Sounds good to me ... see you soon."

The meeting was held at the 'Lions Pit' tavern on Bear Tavern Road, the far western end of Trenton. A nicely, decorated but dim place which resembles a hunter's cabin, safe from the media and the press. People there tend to mind their own business and the one television in the entire place seems to have only one channel—"The Hunter's Station."

Mayor Holmesbrook and I adjourn to one of the tables at the rear of the tavern. A waitress, dressed in a uniform resembling that of a serving winch, brings us our drinks and takes our food orders.

"Hey Brendan ... remind me later to inform you on how I do hate this awful place. It looks like a place you would see in 'Deliverance'."

"I would think you, would appreciate a place off the beat and path. No chance of media or photograph hounds in a place like this. This is as discreet as one could get. So, what do you have to bring our friend down?"

Mayor Holmesbrook pulls the manila envelope from his briefcase and slides it across the table. I take a casual look around the dining room before opening the envelope. I pull out several photos from the envelope and study them carefully. One photograph shows the Councilman in a crowd—a banner in the background indicating gay rights. Another photograph shows him giving a man a hug—whether it's a passionate one or not—its interpretation is ambiguous at best.

Another photo shows the Councilman moving through the crowd with the same man walking behind him, with both hands on each shoulder of the Councilman. Other photos show different angles of the crowd— mostly men—holding signs expressing their prosocial and proactive views on gay rights and gay acceptance. I return the photos to the envelope and slide it back over to the Mayor.

"I had no idea the Councilman is gay. I wonder if his wife knows this. How old are these photos, Martin?"

"They were taken during his senior year of college. A friend of a friend dug them up a couple months ago and thought I would be interested in buying them."

"That would certainly explain why he has been straddling the fence on the healthcare reform regarding gays and lesbians. He does not want to come off as a homophobe; it would raise questions on his personal life and feelings. On the other hand, he doesn't want to be too sympathetic either. Once again … more questions."

"Well, with the country still trying to understand AIDS and religionist still placing the blame on homosexuals, one way or the other, a boat is going to get rocked."

"By the way Martin, what is your stand on this issue? Who are you more afraid of pissing off … the gay community or the religious community?"

"I must admit, this will be a tougher issue than the economy and the environment combined. But I will side with the religionist. And rightly so … if I went the other way, these photos would be meaningless."

"I clearly see your point, Martin but timing is most essential. Spring the trap too soon, the lion will be startled and he will flee … too late and

the lion will have already accomplished its mission … especially with live bait."

"I will spring the trap in the district I am weakest in … the south side. I will give them something to no longer praise Brennan for the takedown of the Griffin."

"So, you do know how to snare the lion. I am very impressed," I say to Martin with a sheepish grin.

"With the south side in my pocket, the west will follow. I already know the east and north side are in my corner. This will bring them all together … I am certain of it."

"A toast then … to another term as Mayor … Mr. Mayor."

We both raise our glasses and finish our drinks in one shot. The waitress brings us our meals to the sound of laughter.

CHAPTER 7

The Mayoral race has begun. Both candidates are fighting fair thus far. It seems as if both parties are waiting for the other to lay down the 'mudslinging gauntlet'. At the present, Mayoral candidate David Brennan has a slim lead in the popularity polls. For Mayor Holmesbrook it is still too soon to hit the panic button.

In the meantime, I continue to play the role of a double agent—or a more suitable term—devil's advocate. Both parties appear to trust my loyalty to each other and questions our friendship not. The other candidates are so far behind in the polls that this has become a race of two.

During this time, the trial of Jeremy "The Griffin" Smith has come to a close. The verdict; not guilty on all counts which included: murder, manufacturing, possession with intent, resisting arrest, assault, and the violation of the RICO Statute—thirty-seven counts in all. Mr. Smith was acquitted thanks to the incredible work by Carson Harding, Attorney at law. This is sure to put a damper on the strategy Councilman Brennan was hoping to use. When he hears about this news he is sure to panic, forcing him to draw 'First blood'.

CHAPTER 8

The election is now only two weeks away. Both candidates had people in their organizations gather information on the other. The proverbial 'mud-slinging' had officially begun.

The Trentonian, a local newspaper ran an article and presented photos of Mayoral Candidate Brennan—photos which created quite an uproar throughout all parts of Trenton. Religious leaders, union reps, and many other interests groups became vocal. David Brennan had become the biggest hypocrite and many experts suggested he should quietly 'bow out' and maybe move to San Francisco.

What the papers, media, and special interest groups didn't know was David had already been 'tipped off' about the photos which gave him time to prepare a defense—and immediately come forward and provide a statement—two hours later.

David Brennan approaches the podium.

"Good morning to all. I realize how disastrous this may seem and it is obvious that my opponent feels he has exposed something which would not only damage my campaign but my morals as well. I am here today to provide you with nothing but the truth to clear my name ... now and forever. There are several points I need to inform you of. First, the man in the photos was my roommate for four years at Trenton State. When you live with and get to know someone for that many years, a friendship is formed. A friendship forms regardless of that person's race, creed, political ideals, and yes, sexual orientation. Secondly, he was a friend who not only knew issues of government but was passionate about all the areas affected by bad politics. This friend instilled in me a special drive; to seek out the truth in politics while being mindful to protect the people in the process. This friend supported my cause and I his. Third, I accompanied my friend to this rally for two reasons. First, I needed to understand his reasons for this particular fight and secondly, to assist my friend. He was diagnosed with AIDS in our sophomore year and at the time of the rally, needed a

helping hand to get around. For instance, the photo of us walking through the crowd with his hands on my shoulders ... I had to use my eyes for the both of us. He was beginning to lose his sight and did not use that as an excuse to miss the rally. For that, I admire and applaud his bravery. And for those who released the photos, they were wrong about the identity of my friend. He is not Peter Matthews, a Wall Street businessman from New York. He is Nicholas Britton, of Lansdowne, Pennsylvania. I would like to apologize to Mr. Matthews on behalf of the mistaken identity and I hope and pray that this mess has not caused you too much grief and discomfort. As for my friend in the photo ... Nicholas has been dead for almost three years now. If you need proof, you will find him buried at the Ewing Cemetery ... take flowers with you, if you should go there. I think he would truly appreciate it as would I. I want to thank the media for coming out and I hope and pray you will do your job by confirming all that I have stated this morning. It's what we call the truth ... thank you."

At the closing of David's statement, what followed could only be labeled as, "Thunderous applause."

CHAPTER 9

The statement given by David Brennan not only cleared his name but drew sympathy and compassion in his direction. David was now seen as a politician with love and respect for others' views. The statement he made was labeled by many as, "Endearing and moving." The Trenton Time, another local newspaper, labeled David as, "A true human with a keen understanding of the human condition."

The Mayor had no defense for this slander and needed someone to fall on the sword. He eventually gave a statement, claiming someone from his campaign received the photos from the Governor's Aide. The Mayor also stated that the person from his campaign no longer works for his campaign. When the Governor heard this news, he immediately fired his aide.

At the closing of his statement, the Mayor regretfully apologized to the people but failed to apologize to his opponent; a move labeled as, "Tasteless," in the eyes of the media. The media had hoped to get a statement from the Governor's Aide but he was nowhere to be found … ever.

It was no longer a surprise that Councilman David Brennan is now Mayor David Brennan. The election was a landslide victory that was not a prediction by the state and the media. You see, Brennan had always been a conservative running in a city predominately, liberal.

The now, ex-Mayor could only offer a half-hearted congratulations to his opponent but everyone could see or sense that deep down, Mr. Holmesbrook would love nothing more than to pour gasoline on David and set him afire. The thing that Holmesbrook found most disheartening, was how so many supporters had jumped ship and one in particular, yours truly. I was nowhere to be seen and even had my address and phone number changed. Holmesbrook probably began to wonder if I had been an infiltrator; me and the still missing Governor's Aide. This was a thought; a feeling he just found impossible to shake.

CHAPTER 10

The new Mayor takes a ride out to the place he always goes when he wants to celebrate or unwind—the ranch out in Cream Ridge.

Going through the usual security checkpoints he enters the room like a knight who had just slain the dragon and will now be rewarded for his unflinching bravery. Guards and waiters seemed to bow lower and longer now. David goes over to his usual spot and awaits his trusted friend and business companion.

"You are a man of greatness and I can only see you becoming greater," my voice resonated from down the hallway.

David turns and spots me entering the room.

"My apologies for not being on hand but I had to double-check things. I wanted things perfect before you arrived."

"It is not a problem at all, my friend. And I do appreciate how thoughtful you have been. I could not have done it without your help. You have always been there for me, whenever I needed you. For that, I am eternally grateful."

"I guess I'll just have to hold you to those words, Mr. Mayor. I do love it when someone is eternally grateful to me."

After pleasantries are made, we both take a seat in our usual place. The waiter brings us drinks and exits.

"I have been watching the news about our friend. He seems to be taking this loss particularly terrible. He doesn't even try to hide his feelings … like some spoiled child who had his bike or 'trick-or-treat' bag snatched from him."

"I believe what hurts him most is your disappearing act with not as much as a 'good-bye' or 'you've been screwed'. Has he given up the search for you or is he still pining away?"

"I trust, he now realizes how royally he has been reamed," I say with a smile.

"And what about our little aide … Any news yet, on his whereabouts, my Master?"

"Oh, someone will find his body in a landfill … two weeks from now. The ex-Mayor will be implicated but nothing will come of it."

"Please, forgive me for asking this but why me instead of him?"

"Holmesbrook was a weak man with the most insipid of ideals. Someone like that could never be my Gatekeeper. He was the type who could be easily bought and lacks that necessary perception I crave in my employees. That fool even forgot who was working for whom. Besides, a weak fool could be forgiven by Him for it is not a sin to be stupid. And because of that, I hope we are clear on what I expect from you."

"We are extremely clear, my Master. Your wish is my will."

"Together, you and I will achieve great things. But you must remain competent and focused. You are with me because your sins are unforgiveable in His eyes. Don't misinterpret what I am saying to you. I only nurture the sin … not cause or create it. Remember … Asphodel is not the worst place in hell for someone to be. And who knows … should you become president you will see what death is like in the land of Elysium."

David nods, finishes his drink and begins to retreat to his room, leaving me as usual, to my thoughts.

Indeed … I only nurture the sin …

Afterword: Lucifer's soliloquy

When are they all going to realize there is nothing special about You? You place these souls in a land and condemn me to serve in that same land. You try to cover up for that mistake by sending them Your son; mistake number two. You tell them they have to believe in You or else. That sounds like a dictatorship to me. They create a tower to reach You and how do you reward them … You give them all different languages. Another blunder by You. You thought by giving them the ability to create different religions, they would become more affable or amiable towards one another but that was another mistake by You.

These poor fools are down here killing each other in Your name. One never hears someone killing in my name. You deceive them by telling them all they have to do is believe in You and they can have everlasting life. So, if a man bashes his wife and child's skulls in with a hammer but believes in You, there

is a place in Your kingdom for him? I think You are a greater deceiver than I. It is so gratifying to continue telling them these things about You. Soon, my army will be complete and I shall return to take what should have been mine from the beginning. And as for You ... I have a very special place for you when this is over ... I promise You this!

END

"As for the head of those who surround me,
Let the evil of their lips cover them;
Let burning coals fall upon them;
Let them be cast into the fire,
Into deep pits, that they rise not up again.

PSALM 140: 9-10

Printed in the United States
By Bookmasters